ABOVE THE HARBOR

a novel

by David Athey

Cover design and interior layout by Taylor Thomas Smythe

Published independently

ISBN: 979-8-363262-09-8

Dear Reader,

A different version of this story was published in 2011 as *Christopher*. I hope you enjoy this revision.

Kind regards,
David Athey

ALSO BY DAVID ATHEY

Art is for The Artist

Iggy in Paradise

Seventy: Flash Fiction Stories

The Count of Trinity

The Glimmering Kid

Eleven Manatees

The Pilgrim

The Straw That Healed the Camel's Back

Hunting and Gathering Heaven

That and This

Danny Gospel

Table of Contents

ABOVE THE HARBOR

Chapter One

Summer of 1993

Christopher Lake awoke late, having spent the night with the aurora borealis dancing in his dreams, a nightmare in which he had to battle dragons and other beasts in the fiery lights above the harbor. The eleven-year-old blamed the bad dreams on Minnesota, because when his family had lived in California, he'd never dreamed at all.

Chris rolled out of bed and shuffled to the open window. The sky was thick with bright chunks of clouds that made him think of bread. The boy's stomach rumbled and he gazed down at the water where the great Lake Superior was sun-reddened like wine. He licked his lips and forgot about the nightmare. Scanning the shoreline near the lighthouse, he saw a large family fishing—casting, reeling, untangling lines. Christopher wondered what it was like to have brothers and sisters, and he felt a jealous ache. A dark thought kissed him and yet the water was so luminous that a smile crossed the boy's face. He whispered, "Maybe I should go meet the girl who lives in a cathedral."

Chapter Two

Terra Corwin lived in a Gothic mansion three miles up the shore. Chris rode his bicycle toward Terra's house, the lake breeze singing happily in his ears while the waves added glad tidings of their own. The road to "the cathedral" was one he already knew, with scenic overviews of rocks and water that seemed ancient and freshly made, a paradox deeply felt if not yet understood, and after several long pauses to contemplate cliffs and water and light, Chris eventually turned into the Corwin's almost hidden driveway, whistling like a bird, or rather squawking, to make his presence known.

The girl ignored him. She was sitting on the front steps, reading a book. Chris squawked again, inching his bicycle closer, unable to keep from staring at the most beautiful person he'd ever seen. It wasn't the blonde hair, or the smooth skin. It was definitely something within.

The girl glanced up, then down at her book.

The boy blurted, "What are you reading?"

She sighed and showed him part of the cover. The title was illuminated with golden hues and said *Medieval* something or other.

"Cool," the boy said. "I like pictures of ruins. I mean, I also like to read. Um, mostly deadly adventure stories."

"You like ruins and defying death. How sweet." The girl laughed, the full weight of the book falling upon her lap. "I'm Terra."

"I'm Christopher. Some people call me Chris. Or Topher. Or Sacramento. My family moved here from Sacramento." He pointed at the book. "Adventure?"

"Well, it's more of a love story. But not fluffy. It's philosophical and theological."

"It's what?" The boy mouthed the words, tasting the possibilities. "Philosophical? Theological?"

Terra lifted the book to her heart and stood on the top step. "I think I'll go inside."

"Wait." Chris propped his bike against the iron railing. "Is it true you've never gone to school? They say an old wizard gives you private lessons."

"An old wizard? You really believe that?"

"Is it true?"

Terra's eyes were as challenging as her voice. "Do you believe it?"

"Sure," he said. "Why not?"

"Well, you see..." She was about to explain about her grandfather, a retired professor, when her mother opened the grand, Gothic door. "Terra? With whom are you speaking?"

The girl paused for a moment, blushing. "I think this boy wants to see the house."

Mrs. Corwin stared at him. "I believe—in fact—I know, you are the Lake boy."

Chris smiled at the lady dressed in black. "I'm one of the Lake boys. My dad is the other. He's the older one."

Terra scoffed at the lame joke, but Mrs. Corwin showed no emotion. "I know your parents from the Club. They seem like fine additions to the Two Harbors area. And I have seen you riding your bicycle along the North Shore. You are always alone."

"I'm not alone now."

"Very well," the lady said. "Come inside the house. We shall give you a tour. Wait. Please wipe your feet."

"Okay. I'll even take off my shoes and socks to see the cathedral!"

"Please leave your socks on. That would be splendid."

"Okay, I'll be splendid," he said, kicking off his shoes.

The first floor of the mansion was nothing special—at least not to the mind of the young visitor—the living room with its French furniture, the kitchen with its Italian counter. "It's a house, all right," Chris said.

Mrs. Corwin led the boy, with Terra following, from the kitchen to a colorful sunroom. The lady in black pointed. "That piece of stained glass is a real Tiffany."

"Spiffany!" the boy replied.

"Excuse me?"

Terra stepped forward. "Library. I think Christopher wants to see the books."

With narrowed eyes, Mrs. Corwin allowed the boy to pass. "Very well. Visit the library and read for a while. It may do you some good."

Up the stairs the boy and girl hurried, side by side, hands almost touching.

The Corwin's library took up most of the second floor, rows of wooden bookcases with volumes in many languages. On the walls between the bookcases were paintings of landscapes and seascapes, animals of mythical proportions, shimmering fish, churches, saints, and lovers.

Terra led Chris to a scarlet loveseat. "Want to sit here and read?"

"Huh?" The boy's attention was caught by a painting

above their heads. Medieval knights were engaged in mortal combat. "Man alive," he said, "man alive," and couldn't stop staring.

"Okay," Terra said, "we can sit someplace else if the painting makes you uncomfortable."

"What? Why would I feel uncomfortable? I'm probably descended from a long line of medieval people."

"Go find a good book," Terra said, "and I'll meet you back here."

"Okay."

The library seemed filled with wall-to-wall miracles. Chris wandered around, browsing happily, and returned with a book of poems by Gerard Manley Hopkins.

"Excellent choice," Terra said.

"I don't know half of these words," he said, staring at one of the poems. "But I like how they taste."

The reverie of reading together in a room constructed to go on forever from world to world made it easy for Terra and Chris to become good friends, connected by some of the highest forms of creativity.

"*The world is charged—*" Chris began.

"*—with the grandeur of God,*" Terra answered.

And there was music. Charged with a grandeur that was simultaneously happy and sad, the music drifted down from the third floor. Chris had never heard Gregorian chant before, and he wondered who was up there singing. He was dying to visit that upper room, and he thought Terra would intuit his curiosity and invite him to the heights, but she just kept on reading her book.

Exactly one hour later, the music stopped.

Terra looked up and whispered, "You better go. Now."

"Right now?" The boy wondered if he'd offended her. *Does she feel I ignored her? Maybe I should've complimented the sheen of her hair or the cleanliness of her shoes.*

"Okay. I'll go," Chris muttered. He hurried over to the stacks and re-shelved the poems.

"You're too late," Terra said. "He's coming down the stairs."

Descending from the chapel, where he'd been chanting his daily prayers, the old professor appeared. He was tall and somewhat wide, stuffed into a charcoal suit. He had a thick moustache slightly yellowed from cigar smoke, but he didn't smell like smoke. Instead, Chris caught a whiff of incense when the geezer sauntered by. The professor didn't seem to be aware that his granddaughter and a boy were in the library. He stared at silver drapes framing a lakeside window, the fabric a suffused luminescence, and flung them open.

"*Lux Christi!*"

Chris grinned, pleased with what seemed to be a game; and he responded with the first word that came to mind.

"Silvenshine!"

"Eh?" The professor turned, surprised by the strange boy and his poetic outburst. "Goodness and graciousness. What did you say?"

"Silvenshine!"

Professor Corwin wrestled with the syllables under his breath, trying to repeat and interpret the playful glossolalia. "Sil...ven...shine. Hmm, indeed. *Et erat lux*!"

"Huh?" Chris glanced at Terra and whispered, "Is that good?"

She nodded. "Very."

Chapter Three

Every day that week, Chris wore his best clothes and rode his bike to the cathedral to be with Terra. He was hoping he'd be invited to climb the final stairs to the chanting sanctuary, but instead, the girl invited him outside for walks in the wildly-tended garden where she loved to point out butterflies.

"Tiger swallowtail! Look!"

"Where?" The boy whirled, his eyes searching, but the tiger had vanished into golden air.

"Christopher, did you see it? That's my favorite butterfly. Talk about amazing, the wings catching so much light. Look over here. Daisies!"

The boy wasn't much for flowers. "Yup, there they are."

"*Daisy* isn't their actual name," Terra said. "Their actual name is so much stronger. Christopher, do you ever think about how words get changed?"

"Um, maybe, I guess, when I'm reading old poems."

"Like the word *goodbye*. It means *God be with you*. In the olden days, every goodbye was a prayer."

Chris wanted to say something intelligent to keep up with her. "Huh," he said. "Huh."

Shaking her head, Terra frowned. "It's sad what happens to language. I've seen it everywhere in the library. New books lack the power of old books. In the old books, people will say, 'God be with you'."

Chris thought about it. "Well, not everyone wants to talk about God."

"I do," Terra said, and became silent.

The boy followed her iconic eyes, contemplating the estate ablaze in zenith sunshine. Chris thought the setting was beautiful enough for the most beautiful words, but no words were beautiful enough for Terra. And yet it was time to say something—because it was time to go home for dinner. He almost said *goodbye*.

Terra picked a daisy and handed it to him. "In the old books, this flower is called a *day's eye* because it stares at God all day."

"*Day's eye*," Christopher said, holding it up to the dazzling sky.

Chapter Four

At sunset on the 4th of July, alone on the hill near his home, feeling sort of romantic and spiritual and not sure what to do about that, the boy made a triangle of twigs and struck a match.

"Cool," he told himself. And he felt, as many have felt, a strong connection between soul and fire. A few minutes later, wanting more, the boy added a branch of hemlock from a tree that had fallen last winter after seven-hundred years of sinking its roots into bedrock.

"Very cool," Chris said, the sparks thrilling the air like comet tails.

When the sparks alighted on the roof of the house, Chris thought they resembled stars or Christmas lights. "Wow. Wow. Uh oh!"

His parents rushed outside, his mother spraying a fire

extinguisher while his father wielded a belt. Before the belt could strike, Chris reminded his father, "You're a pacifist! And your pants are falling down!"

Joe grunted and belted up his trousers, remembering the need to be philosophically consistent. "I will think about your punishment, kiddo. You could have killed us."

With the fire snuffed out by mechanized snow, Val set down the extinguisher and began rubbing her throat. "Ohh, be still my sweet butterfly gland." She was an endocrinologist, a diviner of the thyroid. "Ohh, be still, be still."

Joe was a business consultant, an ex-socialist who'd capitalized on selling merch for the Grateful Dead. Nowadays he spent most of his time with one eye on a PC and one eye on a Mac, making it easy for Chris to run wild.

Val groaned, "My poor little butterfly gland. It's fluttering and fluttering. Ohh, my entire system is off-balance."

The boy really wanted his mother to stay balanced. "Sorry, mom. I won't make any more fires."

"Ohh," she moaned. "My little butterfly wants to fly away."

"Valerie, babe," Joe said, "we have to do the right thing here. Topher needs to learn his lesson." He turned to the boy. "Where are the matches?"

"In my pocket. I can flush them down the toilet if you

want, or—"

"Follow me." Joe led his son to a ledge overlooking the lake. Ghostly sailboats hovered upon the water, positioned for the fireworks celebration.

"Topher?"

The boy gulped. "Yeah?"

"If you're gonna grow up near the wilderness, you need a better understanding of fire."

"A better understanding of fire?"

"Here. On this bedrock, make a circle of large stones. And be careful with your choice of fuel. Don't use hemlock or any pine trees—they give off deadly sparks. You need to be as careful as a priest."

He didn't know much of anything about priests, except that Father Hopkins wrote the best poems. "Okay, Dad."

"Okay," Joe said. "Look! The fireworks are starting. Your simple fire can add to the show."

The boy didn't even glance at the fireworks while gathering stones and maple branches. When that task was accomplished, the boy added birch bark, took a few deep breaths, and struck a match.

"Good," Joe said, nodding, "you're doing great."

Sweet-scented smoke spiraled into the air, reminding Christopher of the incense that his mother burned when she was sad. Chris turned toward the house to see her standing near the picture window, the glass reflecting fireworks rising from the harbor and falling like tears of flame into the dark water.

Chapter Five

Terra and Chris were not allowed to eat or drink in the library. Not a drop of milk or crumb of cookie would ever despoil the sacred books. The library was for devouring words only, so whenever Terra and Chris needed other sustenance, they were welcomed downstairs into the kitchen where the breakfast nook formed another world of comfort.

One day there was apple bread slathered with butter and strawberry preserves, along with steaming mugs of ginger tea sweetened with brown sugar. Mrs. Corwin ejoyed making snacks that smacked of a feast.

"Did you wash your hands?" she asked.

"Yes, Mother."

"Yes, Ma'am."

Terra smiled at Chris. He had a dreamy look on his face, joyful in the supernal presence of simple graces.

"I feel like we're in a book," he said, "a perfect story in a perfect home."

"Perfect?" Terra's eyes began to water. "A perfect story?"

The boy grinned. "Nothing bad can happen in the cathedral." And then he felt like an idiot.

Everyone knew that Terra's father had abandoned his family for adventures in Europe. There was much local gossip about this, but it was hard to think of Terra and her mother as victims because they suffered his absence with such dignity.

Thankfully, Mrs. Corwin ignored the boy's idiocy. "Christopher, may I offer you some more bread and preserves?"

"You're an amazing lady," Chris said, trying to think of the exact right thing to say. He paused for a moment. "God be with you."

His plate was filled again. And he whispered to Terra, "Your mom is like a queen. And you know what that makes you."

"Pudgy," Terra said, "if she doesn't stop baking every time you're here."

"Haha."

"Yes," Terra said, wiping her eyes. "Haha."

Chapter Six

By summer's end, Chris and Terra had spent hundreds of good hours together, mostly in silence, but also in soulful conversation and playful banter. And then she was gone. Terra flew away to Europe with her mother and grandfather, searching the ruins of Christendom to find her father. He was on a sort of pilgrimage or penitential quest to find forgiveness for being an inventor. Victor Corwin had sold patents to corporations and governments and was featured in *Time* magazine as one of the "Top 100 Most Influential People." The day after that article was published, he had a dream or vision that showed some of his inventions being used by terrorists and others for evil purposes. So much pain and suffering—with his name on it.

Christopher received a postcard from Paris, dated

October 1st, with a stamp featuring a saint with a bouquet of roses, that arrived in Minnesota when the trees were all wild with scarlet. The handwriting on the postcard was elegant, suggesting careful phrasing, and the boy carried the postcard into his room before reading it, very slowly, whispering Terra's words:

We are searching and not finding.
Pray for us.
I hope you are well and reading.
Kind regards,
Terra

The day before Halloween, another postcard arrived, this one from Spain.

We are walking the El Camino de Santiago.
Mother and I struggle to keep up with Grandfather.
I believe he could walk all the way to Jerusalem!
Several people have claimed to have seen Father.
Chris, pray for us. Please.
Kind regards,
Terra

The boy wanted to pray. And he wanted to cry. But

all he did was stare out the window at the cold, glowing water.

Chapter Seven

In the dead of November, Chris opened the window wide as it would go. The harbor was a study in gray, a still life of clouds upon clouds, while the lighthouse offered the slightest blink of light. The sixth-grader had decided to stay home from school that day and read a book he'd borrowed from the city library. *SUPERIOR KILLS*. He was enthralled by the powerful deep, and he scribbled in his notebook the names of sunken ships.

The Stranger

Belle Cross

Hesper

Liberty

Oden

The Rebel

When he looked out the window again, the clouds upon clouds had darkened, thundering with snow-lightning falling, a phenomenon some captains had reported moments before their ships went down. Chris stood and leaned outside, staring and shivering while Lake Superior devoured the flashes of lightning.

The grandeur of God? he wondered. *Or something else?*

Chapter Eight

Great mounds of snow hulked up and down the hill and more clouds filled the sky, day after darkening day. On the gloomiest Friday, the boy tromped home from school, reached into the icy mailbox, and felt his heart leap. There was a new postcard—from Portugal—with a stamp commemorating a saint, a queen who seemed to be weeping. Chris's ritual always had him bringing the message to his room before reading and re-reading it, but this time he couldn't wait, taking in the words right there in the drifting driveway.

The world is beautiful, and terrible.
It is getting better, and worse.
No sign of him. See you soon.

Love,

Terra

The word "love" haunted Chris that day and deep into somber December. On the coldest morning, he awoke for school, rubbed his eyes, and saw a flutter of light. *Is there...a bird in my room?*

The light was like a hummingbird, flitting around his head.

"Topher!" his father shouted up the stairs. "You'll be late for school again! C'mon, get with the program!"

"The program?" The boy tried to sit up in bed, groaning, slumping back to the pillow.

"Hurry, or you'll have to walk to school! I'm not a taxi service at your leisure! I have work to do!"

The feathery light was everywhere in the room and everywhere in the boy's head. He closed his eyes and the light remained, fluttering.

"Oh, wait a sec, kiddo." His father got distracted by a phone call that went on and on—and eventually his mother came up the stairs. "Topher, you okay?"

"Think I have a fever," he rasped. "Or maybe a chill. A fiery chill."

"Aww, sweetie." Brushing the hair from his sweaty forehead, she laid her palm upon him. "Be healed. By the power of all good vibes. Be healed!"

Christopher smiled at his mother's blurry image. "I don't think it worked."

"Hmm. I'll make some chai tea—with extra cinnamon and ginger."

"Thanks, Mom. I'm good."

"You're good?" Val rubbed her thyroid, feeling woozy. "You sure?"

"Yeah. No worries. Just need some rest."

"Okay, sweetie."

All day, Chris saw lights flitting around like crystal hummingbirds. He was hungry, starving, but also nauseous, refusing all sorts of things resembling food that his mother left in his room. His strength was gone and his body ached, especially his ribs, the pain rising and never falling, hour after hour.

Around midnight, he overheard his father say, "No, I wouldn't bathe him in essential oils. He's just depressed. It's a Minnesota thing. Seasonal Affective Disorder. SAD. He'll be fine when the sun finally comes out. Or...when that Terra girl returns."

...when that Terra girl returns...

The sun came out the next morning, and Chris's cold face was sopped with fever.

"Aww, sweetie." His mother pulled down the shade, sat beside her shivering son, and eased a lavender-thick towel over his brow. “May all the forces of healing in the universe be upon you!”

The hovering lights and the lights within became so severe that the boy was unable to sit up. Not even for a second. He was burning, burning, freezing.

Valerie Lake, the doctor, did not believe in doctors. Or pharmaceuticals. She would nurse her son back to health with herbs, extracts, and cosmic maternal instinct.

“Babe, it isn’t working,” Joe said. “I’m driving him to Duluth. You need to let him go to a hospital.”

“A hospital?” Val forced a smile. “Topher will get better soon. I have the tinctures all figured out.”

Joe sighed, not merely frustrated but on the verge of panic. “Please. Why not give the hospital a try?”

“Nope. No dang way.” Val stood her alternative ground. “The mortality rate of hospitals is astronomical. Topher is much safer here. I have the tinctures and the vibes to heal him. He’s already responding.”

The boy had fallen into the sleep that had been calling him as if for ages. Down, down, into aurora nightmares, he dreamed of dragons and other beasts and a battle that ended with him dying three days before Christmas.

Deo gratias...

Kyrie eleison...

Hello, Christopher...

Christopher, hello...

Christopher...

Chapter Nine

When he awoke, the day before Christmas, there was a blurry presence in the room that wasn't his mother or father. It was similar, though. Did he have a brother? A sister? He couldn't recall for sure. He blinked his eyes and began to breathe without aching.

Terra sat beside him on the bed. She had a book in her hands, the poems of Hopkins.

Chris began, "*The world is charged—*"

"*—with the grandeur of God*," she answered.

"Terra. Did you just get here?"

She smiled and brushed away a tear. "Twelve hours ago."

"What? Your mom let you stay in my room?"

"Mother was here with me. Along with your mom and dad."

"Oh. Huh." Chris sat up and touched Terra's shoulder. "Tell me about your father. Did you find him?"

"No."

"I'm sorry. I thought you'd find him. I'm really sorry."

Terra nodded, willing herself not to cry. "Grandfather's downstairs having tea with the others. He chanted over you all night."

"In Latin?"

"Yes, and several other languages. It was very serious. He was just about to call our priest."

The boy placed his hand on the book. "But you did bring the priest. Father Hopkins. *As kingfishers catch fire—*"

"*—dragonflies draw flame*, you dork."

Chapter Ten

Christmas morning, Joe and Val Lake were downstairs by the fireplace, listening to the Grateful Dead.

The boy padded slowly down the steps, not expecting much, thinking his presents would be computer stuff he didn't want and herbal supplements he couldn't swallow.

His mother, wearing a purple sari, exclaimed, "Sweetie! Good morning!"

His father glanced up from a laptop. "Son, you haven't been very good this year, but you're getting some cool stuff anyway. Look—open that box. Yep, that one."

Ripping the wrapping paper, hoping against hope to get something he'd really love, Chris had to accept reality. Inside the box was computer stuff. *Unreal*, he thought.

"Thanks, Dad," he said.

The next box was opened with less enthusiasm. The wrapping paper was decorated with green and red Buddha bellies, and inside, of course, were herbal supplements. Big fat capsules impossible to swallow. *I'll flush 'em.*

"Thanks, Mom."

When New Year's Day arrived in a blaze of snowy glory, Joe and Val tiptoed into Topher's room and placed another gift near his bed. The boy had become a sound sleeper since meeting death in his dreams, and so it was almost noon when he awakened to see the shine on the floor. Two shines.

A pair of skis! Yes!!

Chris scooped the skis into his arms and carried them down the stairs. Tripping but not falling at the bottom, he almost poked his father in the groin.

"Topher! Careful! Castration isn't cool."

"This is an awesome present! Can I ski over to Terra's house?"

"No, not yet," Joe said. "You need to practice in the yard before you try to descend the hill. I don't want you flailing uncontrollably across the highway."

"Haha. Flailing sounds like fun."

"Really? Remember the guy that got crushed by a truck? He was struck down like a drunken deer."

"Sweetie," Val said, "if you want to go to the cathedral

today, I'll give you a ride in the Volvo. Volvos are very safe."

"But, um, I don't want to be safe."

Chapter Eleven

In the library, Terra beamed, loving her Christmas present. "A book! Thank you!"

"And a book for me," Christopher said. "Thank you!"

The boy and girl sat on the loveseat and read for a while. Terra's book was *Anne of Green Gables*, and she was constantly bursting out laughing.

Chris looked up from *The Fellowship of the Ring*. "What's so darn funny?"

"This girl—Anne—she's hysterical. I mean, she really suffers from hysteria. But she's so earnest and alive. I like her. She's a kindred spirit."

Chris nodded, pleased that his gift was a source of happiness. "Being earnest and alive is good. And I get that kindred spirit thing."

"Do you?" Terra looked at him in a way that seemed like a kiss—at least on the cheek—and then returned to Green Gables.

Returning to Middle Earth, Chris thought the place was sort of like Minnesota, and he fully believed there could be Ringwraiths on apocalyptic horses in the area.

"Can you hear him?" Terra asked.

"Him?"

"Yeah. He's coming down."

"The old wizard!"

"Don't call him that. He's a man of faith, not magic. And he doesn't even have a beard."

"Oh. Okay."

The professor tromped down the stairs into the heart of the library. "Hello, hello. Happy holy days! How good to see you reading. May I offer you some Aquinas?" He reached for a giant book embossed with golden medieval script.

"Wow," Chris said. "Hey, what happened to your moustache?"

"I gave it to an elvish bat that lives in the rafters of the chapel."

"Grampa! Don't say weird things."

"That's what I told the bat—except I didn't call him Grampa." The professor chuckled and ambled away, lugging the massive book.

"Goodbye," Chris said.

"*God be with you*," the professor corrected. "Do not be so batty. Heh heh."

Terra shook her head, sighed, and whispered, "I'm sorry. Gramps has been acting strange lately. His brain seems a bit off. We might have to bring him to a doctor."

"Oh? My mom's a doctor. Maybe she could help him. She tries to fix my dad's brain, gives him stuff like ginkgo."

"Ginkgo? That sounds like a Tolkien character."

"Yeah. Ginkgo Baggins! The healer hobbit."

"Indeed. A good friend of Anne of Green Goblins."

"Do you mean Anne of Green Mordor?"

"Haha, maybe," Terra said. "Red-haired girls have the Follicles of Power. Beware. They are not to be trifled with."

"Or blondes, either," Chris said, "with follicles like Gollum's calls."

"Not sure what that means," she said, "but you better beware of Blonde Terra, Terror of the North!"

"Yikes," he said, grinning. "I will beware."

"And now begone, mortal one!" Terra accompanied Chris downstairs where he put on his boots and coat; and the kids couldn't stop laughing. "Stop it," one said. "You stop it," the other said. Over and over, they laughed and laughed, and then hushed when they heard the professor and Mrs. Corwin upstairs in the chapel. The adults were chanting—otherworldly words and music rising and descending.

"I should join them," the girl said. "*Adios*."

"*Adios?*"

While Terra hurried toward the stairs, Chris tromped outside into the twilight, carrying *The Fellowship of the Ring*. He loved how the earth looked so mystical, the trees shimmering while rising into shadow. For a moment, he felt perfectly at peace, and then he was suddenly sad, wishing he were in the Corwin's chapel among the otherworldly.

In the morning, after breakfast, the boy strapped on his new skis. *Such a great present. This will change my life. I'm gonna fly*! His parents had forgotten to buy ski-poles, so he used a couple of tree branches for balance, carefully making his way around a mound near the house, the slightest slope allowing him to gain some experience. *I got this*. Grinning with unearned bravado, he turned away from the house and began flying down the hill toward the harbor. *Yes! So awesome! And easy. Like walking on air. Go, go, go! I'll be seeing Terra in no time. How come I never skied before? It's sooo awesome! And easy. Feels like I'm in the clouds. Wow, so fast! Whoa, whoa! Ooohh, crap!*

He couldn't stop at the bottom of the hill, flying into the middle of the road, wiping out with a loud scraping and a moan. He was soon greeted by a man in a pickup truck who honked and angrily swerved, nearly running Chris over. *Like a drunken deer! If I get squashed, that's what my dad will say at my funeral. 'He was a good boy, but a bad drunken deer.'* Not wanting to hear that at his funeral, Chris dragged himself to the side of the road and wondered how many bones were broken.

"Ouch. Ow. Owwoahh."

Two minutes later, a frightened, angry woman in a Volvo appeared, window open. "Get in here. Now! And leave those skis right there in the ditch. You need to slow your life down, mister. When we get back to the house, we're gonna have a serious talk."

"A serious talk?"

"Yes. About meditation."

Chapter Twelve

After meditating with his mom for a boring hour on Grateful Dead yoga mats, Chris bundled up and walked to the cathedral, hoping he'd be invited to join in the mystery of the chapel. He knocked on the great Gothic door, expecting Terra to answer, but the professor appeared and let him inside. "Please remove yourself from those boots, Christopher, and join me in the kitchen."

"Yes, sir."

Visions of baked goods danced in the boy's head—he couldn't wait to sit beside Terra and engage in playful conversation while feasting on sugar. The kitchen was aglow as usual and the table awaited his presence with a welcome of warm cookies. Chocolate chip and oatmeal raisin. Chris had enough manners not to openly drool, but he did lick his lips.

"Sit," the professor said.

The boy gladly obeyed. "This is great. Where's Terra?"

"Upstairs."

"Still asleep? It must be ten by now."

"The time is ten-eleven. Terra is very awake. She and her mother are in the library."

"Oh. Is she waiting for me?"

The professor pulled two mugs from the cupboard. "We should stay in the kitchen. Would you like some cocoa? It is warming on the stove."

Of course the kid wanted cocoa, but he was dying to know what was going on in the library. Christopher shrugged. "I'll drink whatever you're drinking."

"Two whiskies," the professor said. "Coming right up."

"Really?"

"Don't be daft. We will drink cocoa."

"Okay, fine. Will the ladies be joining us?"

"Relax." Professor Corwin hoisted a kettle and poured steaming chocolate to the brim of the mugs. "The ladies are having a serious discussion. It could last until lunch, or perhaps later."

"Later?" Chris muttered. "What on earth are they talking about?"

"Have an oatmeal cookie," the professor said. "These

just came out of the oven. I made them myself. With molasses."

"You made oatmeal cookies with molasses?"

"Please remove the surprised look from your face. Now eat, and drink. No, wait! Will you give the blessing?"

"Um, okay, I'll try." The boy raised his hands toward the high ceiling. "I give unto thee—and also to thou—the blessing."

"Ahem. Amen."

Chris and the gentleman reclined and feasted. And feasted some more. Nobody was counting, but the boy ate five cookies and drank two cups of cocoa, following the example of his host. They dined in meditative silence, tastebuds rejoicing. It was one of the best meals ever, until the sound of crying could be heard upstairs. The boy eyed the staircase, his soul ascending to the bookshelves and through the great stories of love and suffering to comfort his girl.

The professor asked, "Has Terra told you about her father? About my son?"

Chris nodded. "I know a little."

"Well, then I will tell you more." The old man's eyes filled with tears. He took a final sip of cocoa and swallowed it down as if wishing it were whiskey. "Terra's father is like Leonardo Da Vinci, a great inventor. One of the things he invented was the three-dimensional printer."

"Three-dimensional. Far out."

"My son is obsessed with the idea of three. When he was a little boy, he always asked about the Trinity. His face would scrunch up in innocent puzzlement as he tried to figure out how Three Persons could be one God."

The crying intensified upstairs.

"After achieving worldly success, Victor felt guilty. Some of his inventions had become weaponized, fallen into the wrong hands, used for darkness instead of light. And so, he embarked on a life of penance."

"Penance?"

"The word is new to you?"

"Yeah. Sorry." The boy was ashamed of his ignorance. He thought he'd probably get a lecture now about the importance of old books and ancient customs.

Professor Corwin spoke gently, "To do penance is to serve God in a way that hurts the self."

"Like getting a nose piercing?"

"No, more like a piercing through the heart." The professor paused. "A few years ago, Terra's father went on his first pilgrimage of penance. He began in Jerusalem with the *Via Dolorosa*."

"Um."

"The Way of Grief. The path to the Crucifixion."

The boy squirmed in his chair. “Do you believe Terra’s father is still alive?”

“Yes. I believe he is doing penance all over Europe and the Middle East.”

“Terra rarely talks about him anymore.”

“She is hurt by his absence. And embarrassed.”

“Embarrassed? Why? Her dad is a great inventor. She ought to be very proud of him. I think I’ll go upstairs and talk with her.”

“Perhaps you should not.”

“Why?”

“Because you have not been invited.”

“But I’m sure I can help.”

Chapter Thirteen

January brooded in snow, mist, and fog, making the Northland a continuous cloud. Chris felt depressed because Terra wasn't speaking to him. Ever since he'd snuck up the stairs and listened to her private conversation, the friendship had cooled. Three times he'd returned to the cathedral, and all three times the professor had answered the door without inviting him in.

"Sorry, Christopher. Terra is very angry. You crossed a line."

"She was crying. I just wanted to be near."

"Dear boy. You should have waited until you were called."

Chapter Fourteen

April was a melodic month of returning birdsong, flocks descending and adding their voices to the rising chorus of the creek. Wrens, kinglets, warblers, and hermit thrushes all called to Christopher, and he sat on a boulder beside the waterway, singing back to the birds—without words—a song like a humming chant, until all the wings fluttered away. Except for the crows. They claimed the crowns of the pines and cawed wrath upon the boy's head. He laughed, and they increased the volume of their cursing, making it seem personal. "Seriously, crows? Really?"

The forest suddenly fell into stillness. Even the creek seemed hushed. The boy glanced around, sensing the approach of some invisible creature. The presence felt large. *Maybe a bear?* Chris had seen a fat bear in the fall, a sleepy beast that had bumbled into the yard, searching for a garbage container, sniffing at week-old cauliflower casserole, before getting cursed away by the crows.

This was no bumbling bear. *Maybe a wolf on the prowl?* Chris listened for the sound of loping or soft pad-padding of a careful predator. The boy focused on a mixed grove of trees—budding birches, maples, and balsam fir—and saw no large animal. There was just a red squirrel on a high branch, tail twitching as if it had seen a ghost. *In the middle of those Christmas trees. There!* The boy felt the energy of danger. He wanted to run. He also felt drawn to the creature hiding in the shadowed sanctuary. Christopher wanted to know what a wolf knew—its journeys through the boreal forest, midnight songs to the winter stars, and the long loneliness of the hunt.

Two lights appeared, eyes pouncing on air, yet perfectly still. The eyes of a cat. *Look at that!* The boy blinked. He'd seen a tomcat hunting in these woods. But this was no tomcat. And he'd seen a bobcat springing for a bird in flight. That feline was impressive. And yet, this was beyond a bobcat.

It was a lion.

Chris saw its whiskers hungering in a slant of light. Golden ears appeared, bent aggressively forward. It was a mountain lion, breathing steam, apparently trying to decide if the boy was an enemy, a nuisance, or prey.

The crows cawed and cursed, to no avail, then beat their wings for the sky.

Knowing he should flee as well, Christopher stayed, squinting into those fiery eyes, transfixed. The lion stepped out of the Christmas trees. *Holy...yes...* The boy stood, wanting to run across the water and fling his arms around its neck and kiss its killer face. He wanted to risk the whims of the wild and embrace the beast like a kindred spirit if not a king. Chris took a nervous step forward—thinking this had something to do with destiny—and it was nothing but a tail swirling and disappearing into fir trees.

"No way, it didn't happen," the boy's father said at the dinner table. "You imagined it."

Val nodded, chewing seaweed. "We've all imagined things."

"That's for sure," Joe said, laughing. "I once saw a leprechaun leap out of Frisco Bay. Yup. It landed right on the Golden Gate Bridge."

"Thank goddess, those days are over," Val said, reaching for more weed. "Now we see things as they really are."

"I really saw a lion," the boy said, glaring at his plate.

"Well, sure you did," Joe said. "You really saw a lion—in your imagination. Like something you see when reading a story. You were creating it in your subconscious."

"The lion appeared from the Christmas trees," Chris said, looking up from his untouched food. "He was real."

Chapter Fifteen

The next day, with a thrilling chill in the air, Christopher wandered outside in just a T-shirt. His mother shouted after him, "You'll catch your death!"

"My death? I won't catch that again. Not today." The boy stomped back to her and held out his paws. "I'm warm as a lion cub."

Val touched the heat of his hands and frowned. "Lion cub?"

"Grrr," he said, bounding away. "Grr! Grr!"

He returned to the creek and reclined on the boulder, listening and watching in rapture. The creek was awash in small infinities: fiery stones, pebbles, sand, bubbles, and foam, the latter shape-shifting every second into one flowing artwork after another. Minnows slick as moonlight. Trout flashing sunlight. Every round, square, and triangular inch of the creek was a free-flowing masterpiece of the moment.

Murder!

Chris witnessed a murder of crows killing one of their own on the other side of the creek. The injured bird cawed for mercy, and was given no mercy, pecked to pieces. And then a red fox appeared, scaring off the murder with a hungry yelp. He plucked the hapless crow, fangs going red, until the neighbor's dogs arrived—black lab and golden retriever—chasing a small doe. "No!" the boy hollered. "Bad! Bad! Go home! Grr! Grr!" The dogs abandoned the doe, running wildly in another direction, pursuing the fox.

What's wrong with this world? Chris thought, panting. *Everything's hunting everything!*

When he returned from the woods, his mother greeted him warmly on the back stairs. "Guess who came to visit?"

"We have a visitor?"

"Yes, sweetie."

"Who is it?"

"A mother and her beautiful daughter."

"Terra!"

Shivering, Chris hurried into the kitchen where Terra was standing beside Mrs. Corwin. The girl was dressed in green, her mother in black.

Terra lifted a heavy box. "We brought you some presents."

"Awesome," he said, looking at her. "Presents from your travels?"

"No. Grandpa found these treasures in the basement. He thought you'd love them, especially *Orthodoxy* by Chesterton. He said it's time to build your own library."

"Well," Val huffed, "thank you very much. But of course we already have a library."

Trying to keep a straight face, Chris said, "You mean the shelves of books about thyroids and the power of the cosmos?"

"Sweetie, go add your new, um, old and dusty books to the collection. There's room on the bottom shelf."

"Okay." He grinned and turned to the girl. "Terra, can you help?"

"Of course."

And away they went, friends again, just like that.

"You have a gorgeous home," Mrs. Corwin said, gesturing. "I truly love your kitchen. What a wonderful back splash. Is it Venetian? So intricate."

"Oh, thank you. That pattern is from southeast India."

"India. Yes, I always love color in a kitchen."

"For sure," Val said. "Colorful kitchens are very helpful for digestion."

"Really? How interesting. I'd like to hear more about that."

While the mothers talked about colorful kitchens and better digestion over a cup of chai, the kids finished stacking the books and went outside. They sauntered over the rotting leaves from last fall, kicking up the sweet odor of mold and thawing earth. Side by side, the boy and girl traversed into the forest, eventually finding themselves in a sanctuary of pines. The boy stared heavenward. "I think an eagle family nested there in the past."

"But they flew the coop?"

"Wow, Terra. Your jokes are as lame as mine."

The moment he finished speaking, an eagle blazed over the pines, wings whistling.

"Amazing," Terra said. "I really love being here on the hill."

"I love it, too. It's one of the best places in the world."

"One of the best? Not the very best?"

Chris wasn't sure how to answer because he thought the Corwin's property was better. He adored the Gothic mansion with its artwork and library and secret room upstairs.

The girl sensed a muddle in the boy's brain, so she took his hand and turned him north with a gentle tug. "Look at those trees—over there—starting to green."

Quaking aspen buds were trembling to life in the light. Chris smiled, then looked down at the forest floor. He let go of Terra's hand and reached for a blue mayflower.

"No," Terra said.

"You don't want a flower in your hair?"

"Let it grow."

"Your hair?"

"The flower, dork."

Chris liked it when Terra called him a dork, and he happily loped toward the creek. "See the Christmas trees? That's where the lion lives."

"The lion?"

"Grr! Grr! I should have captured him."

"You saw a lion? For real?"

"Yeah, for real. It ran away from me."

"You were lucky."

The boy puffed out his chest. "So was the cat."

"You're such a dork. King of the dorks."

"Whatever. The lion's hair was the same color as yours. And his eyes were like yours."

"The lion had blue eyes?"

"No, I didn't mean that. I meant they glowed."

"In the Christmas trees?"

"Yep." He gestured toward the firs. "Right over there. You believe me, don't you?"

"I'm guessing you probably saw something."

"It was a lion."

"Hmm."

"You don't believe me?"

Terra searched his eyes. "Do you believe yourself?"

"Of course I do."

"Okay." Terra tugged his hand. "Let's go across the water and investigate your claim. We can leap from rock to rock."

"No," he said, slipping out of her grip. "I can't."

"What?"

"I can't be friends with you. Not if you don't believe me."

"Don't be upset," the girl said, walking past him. "C'mon. Let's go look for evidence."

The boy refused to follow her. "I saw a lion!"

"A lion, huh?" Terra heard a breeze hurrahing through the pines while golden light dappled the forest. She took a deep breath and slowly turned to face her friend. His cheeks were flushed and his eyes watery. "Christopher," she whispered, "would you believe me—about everything? Would you believe me if I said I've seen angels in our chapel hovering above the altar?"

His heart pounded. What could he say? He'd never been to church and didn't believe in angels. And yet, there was Terra's face. Were the angels above the altar as beautiful?

"I don't know," he said. "So don't tell me. Okay?"

"Okay. Your loss."

Chapter Sixteen

Early May, on a mild Saturday afternoon, Terra and Chris were reading in the cathedral library when the girl set aside a biography of Saint Joan of Arc, and said, "Want to visit a secret place?"

Thinking she meant the chapel, the boy nodded eagerly. "Let's go."

"Okay, leave your book."

Chris placed the tale of death-defying knights on a side table and followed Terra down the stairs—sadly, not up to the chapel—and out of the house. Beyond the gardens, Lake Superior was a spectacle of brightness, the water like blue and gold fire. They boy and girl walked along the rock-shimmered shoreline, for a while holding hands, and then not holding hands, Terra letting go. "Here. This is it." On the northern border of the property was a cave carved into an elevation of dark stone.

"Far out," Chris said. "I didn't know there were caves on the lake!"

Terra smiled. "I knew you'd like this. The French explorers referred to these places as *purgatories*."

"Seriously?" Chris clambered forward, almost falling. "I can't believe you've never brought me to purgatory before."

"Well, you're here now."

"Wow, I love it," the boy said, blinking, adjusting his sight. "A person could live in here. Just bring me hot cocoa and cookies every so often."

"Um, some people call this The Living Tomb."

"Cool. Perfect name."

"I wouldn't call it a tomb, though," Terra said, entering deeper. "The explorers used it as a safe-haven from storms."

*Haven...heaven...*Chris thought, trying to remember a Hopkins poem. He scuttled to the back of the cave, plopped on a sort of stone bench, and faced the opening of light pouring in. "This place really messes with your mind. It's cold and damp and dark—and so darn beautiful."

"It's unique," Terra said, sitting next to him on the cool stone, her face shining.

Chris wanted to kiss her. He wanted to worship her. And he wanted to run away.

Instead, he stammered, "Did you really see angels above the altar? In the upper room?"

"Angels?" She paused, then pointed at the lake. "Look."

An ore ship the color of rust was pushing through the water toward the harbor to load up tons of iron.

"It looks corroded," Chris said. "I think that ship needs an overhaul."

"You mean an over-hull."

"Good one, Terra."

"Thanks."

The boy grinned. "I sometimes like your jokes. The punnier the funnier."

"Haha. That's sweet."

Sweet...sweetness...

It seemed the perfect moment to kiss her. Chris leaned toward her, and the girl stood abruptly. "We should get out of here. I didn't tell my mom we were leaving the house. She wouldn't approve of us being in purgatory."

"She doesn't need to know. Let's stay in here a while longer."

"No, Christopher." Terra grabbed his hand and pulled him up. "She trusts us."

"She does? Um, good."

"Yeah. Let's keep it that way. C'mon, let's walk along the shore. We might find a treasure on the way home."

Out of the cave, the boy and girl strolled, picking up rocks and pebbles that glowed brightest in the shallows. Eventually their hands were full.

"They're so cold," the girl said.

"They sort of burn," the boy said. "It feels good."

Their eyes met, no more words spoken, and they threw their treasures deeper into the lake.

Chapter Seventeen

Sunday morning, Sabbath beckoning, Chris opened his bedroom window and watched wings of many colors rise above the lake just as a huge golden halo arose from the water, filling the horizon, the whole sky becoming a crown of fire.

Blinking, the boy whispered, "I really want to see the chapel. Today's the day."

Chris got all cleaned up, put on his best clothes, dying to witness the upper-room ritual, but when he tried to close the window, he got distracted again by the lake. He drifted into a daydream full of fresh-water dolphins with sparkling fins of flame leaping into the crown of fire. An hour passed by like nothing, and another hour, the vision deepening, Superior all grandeur, now an actual ocean full of wilder leviathans—or maybe angels—sporting in the water and sky. The morning was suddenly gone.

And Christopher wanted more.

Chapter Eighteen

Sunday afternoon, Sabbath afternoon, Chris went to the cathedral and rang the bell. "Today is the day. I'm ready."

The bell tolled deep, echoing into the heart of the house, but nobody came to the door. The boy rang the bell again, hoping he wasn't too late. After several more minutes of waiting, he was ready to give up and go home, when the door flung open and a woman appeared in a red dress and white apron. She looked like someone from Germany or Switzerland. She said, "Christopher, do you know how to polka?"

"Polka?"

"Yes, it's a dance."

"Hmm, I doubt if I—"

Terra appeared in the doorway wearing a yellow dress and white apron. “Oops. I forgot to tell you. Today is the Spring Fling at the community center. My mom was just talking on the phone with your mom, and it’s okay to join us.”

“A dance? I don’t know. I was thinking—”

Professor Corwin squeezed into the doorway. He wore funny short pants with red suspenders. “OOM pa pa! OOM pa pa! Silvenshine! Silvenshine! Let’s polka!”

“Oh, I don’t know. I was hoping to—”

The professor bobbed like a bird. “OOM pa pa! OOM pa pa!”

Terra grabbed Chris by the hand and led him down the steps—he nearly fell—and she dragged him over to a blue Fiat. “You’ll enjoy the Spring Fling. It’s fun.”

He spoke nervously. “Will other kids be there?”

“I don’t know. Who cares?”

“Will it be a bunch of goofy old people? And us?”

“Maybe.”

“Hmm.”

Terra squeezed his hand. “You’ll love the dance. I promise. Polka is the happiest music on earth.”

The Two Harbors Community Center, when the Corwins and Chris walked through the door, was in fact hopping with happiness. Many dancers were wearing traditional polka attire, the festive colors enlightening the room while the accordion, trumpet, clarinet, drums, and tuba rolled out a barrel of fun. The dance floor was overflowing. Couples in their midnight years were turning counter-clockwise toward childhood again. Terra and her grandfather joined the spiral galaxy of spinners, hoppers, and dippers, leaving Chris and Mrs. Corwin behind.

The two non-dancers sat at a table. It could have been uncomfortable, but then a mug of beer and a bottle of sparkling water appeared. Mrs. Corwin raised the mug and clinked the bottle. "Cheers," she said, and Chris echoed a cheery reply.

The boy chugged the water, fizzy bubbles tickling his throat.

Mrs. Corwin took a frothy sip of Pabst, dabbed her mouth with a napkin, and said, "Christopher, do you like beer?"

"I don't know," he replied. "Probably."

"What do you mean, probably?"

He gestured toward the patrons at the bar. "Seems like most people like beer. I'm probably the same as them."

"Oh no, Christopher. You are not the same as them. You are very different."

"Well, I'm in no hurry to start drinking or smoking anything. My father used to drink and smoke—and he saw leprechauns."

"Oh my." The woman sipped her beer. "Indeed. Stay away from leprechauns."

The band played the *Chicken Dance* and Chris was intrigued by the spectacle of Minnesotans flapping their arms. He noticed the smile on Mrs. Corwin's face and he blurted, "I'll bet you miss your husband."

Her smile remained but her eyes saddened.

The boy wished he'd kept silent and chugged his sparkling water.

"Hey!" the bandleader shouted, "Is everybody happy?"

There was a joyful noise of shouts, whistles, claps, and stomps. The accordion began a laughing melody—*Stella at the Wheel*. Chris yearned to dance into that sort of happiness. He wondered if Terra would teach him. She was having such a great time spinning around with her grandfather. Had she forgotten about him? The boy began to sweat, feeling the stress of being a wallflower. He thought he'd excuse himself to go to the bathroom, and then make a run for it. His house was only a few miles away, an easy jog. "Um, excuse me," he said, standing to make his getaway.

"OOM pa pa! OOM pa pa!"

Terra and the professor appeared, their faces flushed and glowing, puffing for breath. Terra playfully chided her mother and Chris, "Why aren't you two dancing?"

Blushing, staring at the floor, the boy said, "Um, I

have two left feet. And neither one of them knows how to dance."

"Haha. C'mon, you dork. You'll learn fast. No matter how many feet you have, they can do the polka."

"Okay, I'll try."

Chris stepped on Terra's feet a few times, until his body picked up the pulse of the band. The trick was to follow the heartbeat of the booming tuba and ignore the gypsy-quick accordion. It also helped to let Terra do the leading, at least for the first two songs. After that, Chris led her around the busy dancefloor, careful to keep his feet somewhat under control. He didn't know what he was doing, exactly, except for making his best friend happy and making himself happy in the process. The final dance was the *Kissing Polka*. While it was playing out, Chris didn't think about the words. He was too busy floating through the air with the prettiest girl in the world. When the song ended with a final blast of the trumpet, the dancers all exchanged a kiss. Including the two kids. A quick touch of the lips. It just sort of happened in the flow of the moment.

Mrs. Corwin noticed the kiss, and flinched, almost spilling her beer. "This boy," she muttered, "is going to hurt us."

Chapter Nineteen

Although Mrs. Corwin was wary of Christopher and his future purpose with them, she did not disallow his visits. The boy continued to read with Terra in the library and go for walks outside. One day in early June, the kids were reclining near the lake, not far from the purgatory cave, having just finished a conversation about death-defying knights in the Middle Ages, when Terra reached into her tote bag and handed Chris a gift. "Here. An early birthday present."

It was a beautiful hardcover book. *The Cloud of Unknowing*.

"Thanks. But my birthday isn't until September."

"I know very well when your birthday is."

"Right." The boy held *The Cloud of Unknowing* to the

sky. "Wow, this looks awesome. I can't wait to read it."

"Read some of it now," she said. "Just open up a random page."

Random page? Books have random pages? Chris opened the book and read out loud, "*And so, humbly trust the blind stirring of love in your heart. Not your physical heart, your will.*"

A lone seagull cried above the lake while the boy asked, "Is *The Cloud of Unknowing* a love story?"

Terra ignored his question. "Summer will be over soon," she said, "and you'll be back in school. Are you excited about seventh grade?"

"Haven't really thought about it," Chris said, closing the book.

"You'll be a teenager. Think about it, about growing up."

"Yeah, we're getting so old. Watch out! Here comes that bird."

The seagull fluttered above them, screeching for food.

Terra sighed. "I wish we had bread for her."

"I wish we had bread for us," Chris said, stomach rumbling.

Hovering, begging with its eyes, the bird let out a vicious scold.

"I'm sorry," Terra said. "We don't have anything for you. You'll have to forgive us."

Screech!

"Can't you dive for minnows?"

Screech!

"Go fishing. You have a great lake full of food."

Screech! Screech! Screech!

Terra tried to wave the gull away. The bird fluttered wildly and continued its ravenous demands. Terra raised her other hand and clapped loudly. It didn't work. The bird screeched louder, perhaps playing a game, or maybe it was crazed.

Trying to help the situation, Chris tore out part of a page of *The Cloud of Unknowing* and offered it to the open beak. The gull ripped the paper from his hand and wheeled out over the waters, not chewing on the words but carrying them away as if making an important delivery.

Chris turned to Terra and gave her a grin.

She punched him in the chest.

"Ouch."

"How dare you!" Terra said. "That was a collector's edition. My grandfather bought it in London, years and years ago, long before you were born."

"Sorry. I'll make it up to you."

"What about my grandfather?"

Rubbing his chest, the boy said, "I'll make it up to him, too."

Her eyes demanded penance. “How?”

He winced. “I don’t know. I’m sorry. You’ll have to forgive me.”

“Forgive you?” The girl’s face was all fierceness. “I forgive you. Yes. But I’ve about had it with you.”

Chapter Twenty

Six days of creation, six days of destruction, a week of hell.

Chris phoned Terra to inform her, "My family's moving to Duluth. Um, today. I probably should have told you sooner."

The girl said nothing. She already knew.

"Don't worry, Terra. Duluth isn't far away."

"It's twenty-eight miles."

"Is that all? I can ride my bike."

"Whatever," she said icily. "Don't kill yourself on my account."

Chapter Twenty-One

The Lake family moved to the east end of Duluth where some of the best architecture in the world—Greek, Roman, Tudor, Renaissance, Victorian—formed a neighborhood that didn't seem Minnesotan. Their house was a Tudor that stood half-way up the hill with a partial view of Lake Superior.

On the other side of the street were the Ruins—a large stone archway from a demolished school—the remnant sandstone a dark shade of terra cotta.

The boy couldn't understand why his parents wanted to live in the city. His father could work anywhere with his computers, and did his mother really need so many patients? Her thyroid business had picked up the moment they'd arrived, as if most Duluthians were feeling a bit sluggish.

Terra danced in his mind and he hoped she wouldn't become a mere memory. He sent her an email, saying, "Friends forever." He waited a day. She didn't answer. He sent another email. "Friends eternal." She didn't answer. The third email, although motivated by friendship, was a philosophical slip-up. "C'mon, Terra. Answer, you dorkess."

No reply. And that was that.

Summertime should have been glorious in a city full of blooming gardens and wilderness parks with great gorges and waterfalls, but for a boy out of love, it was all melancholy and gloom.

Chris started watching television.

He slouched on the couch, staring blankly at the comedies, never laughing, and staring blankly at the tragedies, never crying. He started eating junk food, especially potato chips and soda pop. The boy bought them at the gas station and snuck them into the basement. Crunching and slurping, zombie-surfing from channel to infernal channel, Chris soon became sick.

In his sickness, he began to watch soap operas.

Even worse, cable news.

"Topher," his mother said one day, appearing in a fuchsia sari, "what are you watching?"

"Nothing."

She stepped closer. "Is there any good news?"

The reporter reading the teleprompter said, "There is no evidence that red yeast rice does anything to reduce cholesterol levels."

"No evidence?" Val was ready to explode. "She's reporting a study funded by the pharmaceutical companies! That's not journalism! That's propaganda!"

The next day, the cable was removed—actually cut away from the house.

"Take that, propaganda," she said, not realizing Joe had already called for a repair. However, to celebrate her victory, Val gave her son a lavish abundance of seaweed and sprouts. The boy was grateful. His strength returned and he began to spend more time outside exploring the nature preserves. He found sanctuaries in the gorges with pools of cool water shadowed by old-growth pines that had eluded lumberjacks by growing on dangerous ledges. And he climbed out of the gorges, almost to the clouds, contemplating Duluth from above the harbor. Lake Superior, the greatest of waterways, was graced with colorful sailboats breathing new life into his sails; and he thought of Terra again, musing on the good memories, and thinking he could sail to her house.

"I'll sail on my bike, and she'll be thrilled to see me. Friends forever and eternal."

At first light in the morning, Chris jumped on his bike and set sail, holding an open umbrella to gain extra speed. "I'm a genius," he proclaimed. Flying through an intersection, the genius didn't see the rusty '73 Firebird that clipped him and flung him into a lilac bush. While the Firebird continued down the street, Chris wondered if Terra would swoon—or at least be somewhat impressed by his gallantry. The boy even hoped his leg was broken, thinking that would garner more sympathy.

"Augghh," he moaned when a Good Samaritan arrived. "Augghh. My leg. Look. I broke it for a girl."

The homeless man carefully examined him. "No legs are broken. You have some scratches that might become bruises. Now pick up your bike and walk home."

"Walk home? I can't carry my bike up the hill."

"Well, um," the Good Samaritan said, "if you don't want your bike anymore, I'll take it off your hands."

"Fine. Take it."

"And the umbrella?"

Sigh. "Yep, it's all yours."

Chapter Twenty-Two

Duluth hosts one of the world's greatest races, Grandma's Marathon, and Chris, when he was healed, walked down by the lake to watch the runners bless the scenic route with their sweat. He was most amazed by the Kenyans who seemed to run without running. They seemed to dance forward on floating air, and they won all the prizes.

Inspired by the Kenyans, the boy decided he'd run to Terra's house. "Not sure if I'm a genius," he told himself, "but if I just do the work, I'll reap the results."

His first labor was to launder his athletic socks, gym shorts, and a white T-shirt, adding chlorine-free bleach to bring out extra shine. He then ate a perfect balance of protein (egg whites from free-range, organic chickens) and complex carbohydrates (organic flax-oat muffins) and then he went to sleep before sunset, tossing and turning for a while, until he eventually drifted into a dream...running on water...sinking...sinking into Superior...deeper...and deeper into a welcoming light...in the cathedral...in the chapel...

Just before dawn, his eyes flashed open and he leapt out of bed. *This is it*, he thought, lacing up his shoes. *My best chance to make things right with Terra*.

Chris began his personal marathon by walking across the street to the Ruins. He stood beneath the dark archway until it caught the start of sunrise; and away he went, ambling down the hill. Tischer Creek added music to his descent, and he continued—perhaps a little too fast—across Superior Street and veered north on the sidewalk while barely avoiding a man walking a golden retriever. Chris raced along the fence of the Congdon Estate, famous for its obscene wealth and murder. He thought about how Terra's Gothic house was both grand and somehow humble, the perfect structure.

Perfect. So perfect. The first few miles of the marathon were easy, a cool jaunt in the suffused glow of the sunrise. The boy's legs were happy. His lungs were happy. His heart was ecstatic, and he felt like he could run to the heavens. Chris rounded the bend at the Lester River and was greeted by the everyday star rising out of the water. The direct light was nourishing, empowering, and the boy began sprinting near Brighten Beach and its glistening boulders, and he suddenly had a decision to make: Expressway or Scenic Drive.

"Scenic Drive, every time," he said, grinning.

Up Highway 61, sung into legend by Bob Dylan, Chris ran above the lake, feeling weightless while listening to waves rolling upon the shore. Five miles into the journey, the forest near the road began to thin. Houses and yards appeared, and he saw cottages for rent that were painted pink and orange. They seemed so out of place, making the boy laugh. "Did I take a wrong turn—all the way to Florida?" After laughing, Chris realized he was in pain. To fight it, he daydreamed about sailing with Terra in a homemade canoe to a tropical island. He imagined life among palm trees, an epic of sunshine, a kingdom of easy living.

"Ouch. Ouch!"

At the seven-mile mark, his legs and lungs were in agony. The boy stumbled forward and began sweating profusely. He tried to imagine sailing away again, but his mind was bound to the ground, focused on every painful step. The suffering made him face reality, made him think about what was likely to happen if he made it to Terra's house. If he wasn't barfing on the steps, what great words would he say when she appeared? "Auggh, auggh, can I use your bathroom?"

"Yes," she'd probably say, "you stink, dork. Take a shower."

And whose clothes would he wear after showering? Chris imagined himself in a pair of her grandfather's trousers, or perhaps his polka outfit.

"How...can this...end well?"

The boy stumbled along for another mile, pained by everything that Terra might say. She might even sass him in Latin. And he wouldn't know how bad it was.

"You...need to...stop," he told himself, realizing that his flesh had gone all goosey and he was shivering.

Heat stroke, he thought. *I've overheated into chills. Pushed myself too far.*

Chris was wrong. It wasn't heat stroke giving him shivers. It was Lake Superior with a change of wind, a northeastern breeze blowing down from Canada with a great ghost of clouds. Trembling, the boy forced his legs to carry him toward Terra, hoping that she'd be forgiving and welcoming.

A sopping rain began to pour, and the wind gusted against him like slaps and punches, pounding his body to the bones. Chris ran blindly, barely feeling the road, past Stony Point Drive with its wave-misty boulders that would have been a perfect place for a rest in good weather. But now nothing seemed good. The boy careened through the freezing rain as if daring it to kill him, and daring his own body to kill him. Eyes half-closed, he made himself believe he was just a mile from the cathedral—so close to the warmth and mirth he once knew.

He coughed and sneezed. "Almost there...almost there..."

Staggering into a dark corridor of pine, Chris could barely whisper, "No...can't be. This place...only half-way."

It was a café famous for its smoked fish. Smoky Angler's Café. His mother had warned him about this place. "The smoking process makes the fish carcinogenic," she'd lectured. "Just like any form of smoking, this will kill you. Do you want to die for a hunk of incinerated trout?"

"Yepperoo," Chris had said, drooling.

The boy now stood in that memory, in a murderous storm, on the verge of collapsing, hoping the café was an illusion. His knees were shaking, and he spit. "I must be... farther than...halfway. I should've passed...this place...ages ago. This can't be...real."

And yet, if the café was really there, he could spend the emergency money in his sock. He could eat some fish (and bread and cheese) and drink some water. Strengthened, he'd be able to conquer the blasted weather and get to

Terra's house by dusk.

Chris accepted Smoky Angler's as a real place. "Please... don't fool me," he said, staggering to the blurry door.

Chapter Twenty-Three

Ten soggy dollars was enough for a smoked-fish sandwich and a bottle of spring water. Chris slouched at a table near the window, chugged his water in one great gulp and devoured the sandwich in three chomps. The boy was impressed by how quickly he felt strong again. He was ready to roll, but he decided to give his gut a few minutes to settle before returning to the road.

"This ain't the place!" a boy exclaimed, flinging open the door.

A family of three entered the café. Chris looked them over and figured they were from the Twin Cities, on their way to a summer cabin. The mother, in dark sunglasses, reassured her teenaged son, "Yes, this is the place."

The kid wore a maroon sweater and hissed, "This ain't

the same as last year. Where's the aquarium? Where's the eels?"

"We aren't bringing eels to the cabin," the father said. He stepped up to the counter and asked the manager, "Does your trout have bones?"

"Yes, sir. All fish have bones."

"Fine. Give us three-and-a-half pounds. To go. And a loaf of bread. And a pound of cheddar."

"Sharp?"

"Sharp as a bone," the father said. "Bahaha!"

"Nice one, Dad," the boy muttered, "one of your best." He grimaced at Chris. "Dude, you're all wet. What happened to you?"

"Oh, I don't know. I'm sort of on a quest."

"Like Jonny?"

"What?"

"Jonny Quest. It's a cartoon."

Chris shrugged. "Um, sorry, I don't know much about cartoons."

The kid invited himself to sit at Chris's table. "You look sick. What sorta quest you on?"

"Oh, you know," Chris said, "the usual—like a knight."

"Battling dragons?"

"Well, um, I had to battle the weather. It's been brutal."

"Weather doesn't count as a dragon, you freak. You're

like the worst knight ever."

"Connor," the mother called out, "they only have twelve-ounce cans of Dew."

"Then get me two of 'em. Freak." The kid stood and smirked at Chris. "Smell ya later, Sir Sweatalot."

"Oh, probably not. Nice to meet you, though."

The family gathered their food and drinks and exited the café, leaving the manager to shake his head at the good riddance. The manager seemed ready to say something snarky when a car honked outside. Chris flinched and looked to see the Corwin's Fiat almost hit Connor who had wandered onto the road slurping a Dew. Mrs. Corwin honked again for good measure and continued south toward Duluth—with Terra in the passenger seat.

Chris waved. "Hey! Stop! Please stop! Terra, come back!"

The Fiat disappeared.

"That's it," he muttered, trembling angrily. "I'll never try a quest again. Not even for eternal friendship. Not when everything's against me."

"Hey, kid," the manager said, approaching the table. "You can use my phone to call your parents for a ride. Or else I'll call the cops for you."

Chapter Twenty-Four

Dragonflies drew flame through the sunshine, while Chris limped into the shadow of the Ruins. He sat beneath the archway and imagined ancient civilizations, the history of a sorrowful world. *What happened to all those people? Greeks. Romans. Anglo-Saxons. Kings. Queens. Knights. Maidens.* "Dead and gone," he said. "So what's the point?"

Dragonflies sparked their way over the archway and into the blue.

Chris had been grounded, forced to remain within eyesight of his parents' house. So he spent every day at the Ruins, sometimes going without food and water, sometimes eating wild raspberries and drinking from the sky. Neighbors pointed at him and whispered among themselves; and he thought he heard words like "weirdo" and "dimwit" and "vagrant." While grounded at the Ruins, the boy learned to be still, to watch and wait for God knows what—witnessing the clouds turning blood-red at sunset, gorged like some grand catastrophe of grace.

One starry, starry night in July, Chris knelt to see a dewdrop on a blade of grass become a double galaxy.

"Topher?" his mother called out the door. "Are you over there?"

"Yeah," he answered. "I didn't run away."

"Come home. Now." Val closed the door and turned on the outside light.

An hour later, the boy approached the light simultaneously with a luna moth. "Poor thing," he said, knowing the luna would never see the moon's full cycle. And yet, the seraphic eyes on the wings seemed like a glimmer of something immortal. Chris admired the moth until midnight, when his father opened the door and the wings disappeared. "You're not grounded anymore," Joe said, yawning. "Now go to bed. Unless you want to be grounded again."

The next morning, heart pounding, head hungering, the boy decided he'd visit a public library, the one on Mount Royal. It was a perfect day for a walk, clouds like kingdoms allowing plenty of sun. Chris had just begun his climb up the hill toward the building of books when he was struck by a sort of vision. Standing on the sidewalk was a girl in a blue dress.

She spoke gently to the boy, "Are you lost?"

"I, um..."

"Are you new to Duluth?"

"Ahh, sort of."

"You'll be attending Woodland Middle?"

"I don't know."

"You don't know?" She laughed and pointed at the building. "Well, that's Woodland—if you live around here."

"Um, okay."

The girl laughed again. "You seem really lost."

"I'm Christopher," he said, walking up to her. "I live by the Ruins."

"Hi." The girl extended her hand.

Chris kissed it. *Whoa—what am I doing?*

"I'm Mary Joan Mudgett," she said, pleased by the hand kiss and also confused. "Um, my uncle teaches at this school. Your school, maybe. Um, I was helping him decorate his room for the fall."

"The fall," the boy muttered, "already?"

"Soon," Mary Joan said, turning and walking away. "Very soon."

Chapter Twenty-Five

In the fall, on the first day of school, the boy found himself at Woodland Middle, seated behind the girl in the blue dress. The second day of school, he was hoping she'd be wearing the same thing, because that was how he imagined her essence, her true nature. Chris knew he was a bit out of touch with her reality, and of course Mary Joan wore other things through the days and weeks, all of her clothes seemingly homemade, but not dowdy—more like costumes, some of them with puffy sleeves, bright sashes, and glitter. The girl was secure and unique, larger than life in the seventh grade. She even convinced him to play a part in the school musical. He was the Mute Minstrel in love with The Huntress (played by Mary Joan) and during a dance number the boy tripped and made the audience roar.

Everyone thought he'd done it on purpose. His red face became the memory poster for *Out of the Woods*, and all that year he felt obliged to play the clown for everyone. He was good at clowning, and yet not satisfied. *More, more, more* was his mantra, and yet he didn't know what he wanted, but of course he knew what he wanted, but he didn't know...

The eighth grade was more of the same: a comedy of pubescent errors. One day in February, Chris was in the restroom when he noticed that someone had placed a Bible tract on the urinal. It was homemade, colored with crayon. The boy picked it up and read the title: *SAVE YOUR FLESH*.

"Save it for what? A rainy day?"

Chris put the tract in his pocket and decided to ask Mary Joan for a date. He approached her in the lunchroom where she sat with a group of girls. "Hey," he said, trying to be totally cool but unable to look her in the eye. "Wanna grab a Caribou?"

"She prefers antelope," a friend quipped.

The boy's cheeks burned. "Ma-mary," he tried again, "I'd like to grab you—I mean—us grab a Caribou. I mean... coffee."

"NO," she said.

Chris felt the urge to flee, but two of his buddies came up behind him to add support. George had a monstrous nose, tiny eyes, and brown hair sticking up like antlers.

Everyone called him Moosehead. The other kid had a streak of gray in his black hair. His name was Lonnie and everyone called him Skunk.

Moosehead snorted, "Go for it, Sacramento."

Skunk stammered, "Yeah-yeah, ask her."

Chris focused on the crucifix gracing the upper cut of Mary Joan's dress. He cleared his throat, "Ahem. I wa-nanna Caribou to grab us coffee. I mean—"

"NO."

"Hahahaha!" Mary Joan's friends communicated that it was time for the boys to retreat.

It wasn't until the end of eighth grade, in late springtime, when Chris had the courage to approach that table again. Moosehead and Skunk followed closely behind, hoping Sacramento could talk his way into a triple date.

"Okay," Mary Joan said, before the question was even asked. "I'll go to Caribou Coffee with you."

Moosehead snorted, "Me, too?"

Skunk stammered, "Us-us, too?"

"Huh? What? Huh?" Mary Joan's girlfriends were shocked. "All of us? A group date?"

"No. Just me and my dance partner."

Chris grinned and bowed, happily mute.

Chapter Twenty-Six

A good walk has a mystical feel, and for Chris, walking up the hill with Mary Joan was a festival of heavens at play—mysteries playing the earth for all it was worth—a bumblebee ringing in a bluebell, a squirrel waving its tail like a conductor's baton, and a red-crowned sparrow singing like a king of music.

Mary Joan also sang out, "Wildflowers are everywhere! The free gifts of May! Isn't God wonderful? Isn't God colorful?"

The boy nodded, not sure if that was deceptive. He wanted to affirm her belief, without pretending he fully shared it. However, he had the Bible tract in his pocket—*SAVE YOUR FLESH*—for good luck.

Mary Joan walked in her latest blue dress as if the whole

earth had been formed to accentuate her curves, making Chris want to run away to Lake Superior and throw his body into the icy water. And he also wanted to wrap his arms around the girl's lushness and kiss her warmly.

With those two impulses battling for control, he kept stumbling at Mary Joan's side, hands in his pockets, mumbling things like, "Uh-huh, um, yep, yep, okay, yeah, um, uh huh."

When they arrived at the coffee shop, other teens were already crowded into the booths, slurping hot and cold drinks. Boys on one side of the shop, girls on the other. When they saw Chris and Mary Joan, they whispered, intrigued by the sight of a couple that might be flirting with the realm of romance, that sacred world of love, sweetness, and danger.

"Maybe we should go," Chris said, "someplace else."

"Why? The line isn't long. It'll be our turn soon."

The boy paused, frozen by the whispers. He didn't want to lie, and he didn't want to tell the truth about his embarrassment. So he said, "We could stay here. Or we could go back in time."

Mary Joan smiled. "Go back in time?"

"Yeah," he said, nodding to the door, "to that new place."

She laughed sweetly in his face. "It's new? And yet back in time? What on earth are you talking about?"

The eavesdroppers also wanted to know what on earth he was talking about. They leaned from their booths and listened closely.

"Let's go to Old Hound Dog," Chris said.

Moosehead panted, Skunk barked, and several others in Caribou joined the doggie chorus.

Mary Joan rolled her eyes. "Oh, please. Let's get out of here."

"After you, m'lady—back in time we go."

Old Hound Dog was an ice-cream shop decorated with larger-than-life posters of James Dean, Marilyn Monroe, Frank Sinatra, and other such stars. The shop was popular among college students and retirees, the whole place centered on a glittering jukebox that was currently playing *Blueberry Hill*.

The boy sort of danced near the jukebox, sort of tripped, and said, "Mary Joan, do you need to let your mom know?"

She nodded. "I'll call her right now. She'll be thrilled to meet us here."

Oh, nooo.

Mrs. Mudgett had dreamed of being a Hollywood actress, but had settled for parts in the community theater, along with directing Christmas and Easter pageants. When Mary Joan phoned and reported the change in venue for the "non-date," her mother exclaimed, "Ohh, good! I love that place!"

"Settle down, Mom. It's my non-date, not yours."

"Well, then. Maybe I won't show up at all. Perhaps your non-date can drive you home in his non-car."

"See you soon."

"Tee-hee, cutie."

"Bye, Mom."

Chris and Mary Joan checked out the songs in the jukebox, selected a few, then sat on checkered stools at the counter and waited for someone to take their orders. Eventually, an Elvis-looking guy appeared, his apron splattered with a dozen flavors of ice cream. He smiled as if offering the world. "Whatcha want? Name it, ya got it."

"Neapolitan! Three scoops in a sugar cone!" That's what Mary Joan wanted. And Chris, with his stomach rumbling nervously, said, "The same, um, please."

Elvis nodded and strutted to the freezer to scoop up the goodies.

"This is awesome," Mary Joan said, spinning around on the checkered stool. "It's a merry-go-round! Whooeee!"

Multiple thoughts whirled in Chris's brain, all mixed up in a mess of adrenaline, shame, and desire.

Mary Joan is acting different.

She's not who I thought she was.

She's wilder.

Hmm.

Maybe I like wilder.

Everyone's staring at us.

I wish Mary Joan would stop spinning.

Elvis will kick us out.

Her dress is rising while she spins.

Look.

Look at those legs.

No. Don't look.

Fix your dress, Mary Joan. Fix your dress.

No. Let it go.

It's perfect.

"Stop that," Elvis said, arriving with the ice cream.

"Okay," the boy said, blushing.

"I meant her—stop spinning."

"Whooee!" Mary Joan grabbed her sugar cone, waited for Elvis to leave them alone, and pointed it at the boy's heart. "I knew you were different."

"Me? How am I different?"

"You're a deep thinker." The girl paused, nodding proudly as if taking some credit for his soul. "You're not like the other boys in school. Last week in the caf, I heard you debating Skunk and Moosehead about the city's proposal to build a new zoo that would rival San Diego's."

"Yeah, well, wild animals shouldn't be caged. I'm totally

against a new zoo. Or an old one."

She smiled. "You also said Duluth shouldn't compete with California. You said Duluth shouldn't get too big for its britches."

Was there a double meaning in that? Had she noticed his britches?

"Hmm." Mary Joan's eyes narrowed. She focused on his jeans. "What's that in your pocket?"

The boy was horrified. "My pocket?"

His horror increased when Elvis and others began staring, waiting to see.

"What is it?" Mary Joan asked.

The boy's cheeks burned. His whole body burned. He followed Mary Joan's line of sight from her pure green eyes to his pants.

"How interesting," Mary Joan said, looking at the Bible tract. She could only see part of it, the crayon-red proclaiming: *SAVE YO*.

"That's right!" Chris reached into his pocket, grabbed the tract and raised it high above his head. "*SAVE YOUR FLESH!*" he shouted to everyone. "For the love of God, *SAVE YOUR FLESH!*"

Mary Joan's eyes grew wide, surprised by his religious enthusiasm, while Elvis tsked and shook his head. "Man, don't be preachin' in here. Some customers don't dig it."

One customer stood in the doorway, trying to decide what to do. Mrs. Mudgett hadn't expected her daughter's non-date to be so evangelical. She called out, "Time to go, dear! C'mon, now. We don't want to worry the goats."

Chapter Twenty-Seven

On the last day of school, when the bell of freedom sounded, Mary Joan appeared at Chris's locker and said, "I'd like to take you to the Barn."

"What? Take me where?"

"The Barn Theater is having a film festival next weekend. My mother and I are going, and I thought you'd like to—"

"Heck yeah, I'll go to the Barn with you."

"Saturday night is a double-feature," she said, doubly happy about the idea of movies with Christopher. "Both films were shot in Minnesota. The first one's about pioneer farmers and the second one's about star gazing. Sound good?"

"Sounds very good!"

"Great! It's a non-date. And no preaching."

"Okay, it's a plan."

Mrs. Mudgett picked him up in a white Mustang and drove fast while singing songs from various musicals, ending each song by giving herself applause, causing some swerving.

"Mother! Both hands on the wheel!"

Chris wasn't too worried about the swerving—Mrs. Mudgett drove the car better than he rode a bike—and he gazed calmly out the window, until the volume increased with *The Sound of Music*. The chaperone lifted her arms to invite the kids to sing the chorus, causing the car to almost experience the sound of crashing.

"Mom! I'm serious!"

"Tee-hee, cutie pie."

"Mom, you want to see the movies or not? If you don't drive safe, we're going home."

"Hrrumph," she answered, "hrrumph."

The boy was intrigued by the Mudgett family. He'd known some farmers before, but they were stereotypical. How on earth did a person like Mrs. Mudgett fit in the world of agriculture?

"We've climbed every mountain!" she sang. "And now we're here! Let's grab our tickets to the greatest show in the north!"

The entrance to the Barn was studded with Christmas

lights. About twenty people were waiting in line.

Chris had brought enough money to pay for himself, Mary Joan, and her mom. He reached into his pocket, but Mrs. Mudgett would have none of that chivalry.

"This is my treat," she announced. "MOO-vies in a barn! MOO-vies in a barn!"

"Mom," Mary Joan whispered, "shh."

Unable to shh, Mrs. Mudget mooed at the man behind the haybale counter. "Three MOO-vie tickets, please!"

"Um, yes, okay. Enjoy the films."

"Films? Oh no, this isn't a film festival. This is a MOO-vie festival."

"This is definitely unique," Chris said. He took Mary Joan's hand and led her up the creaking, wooden stairs. Mrs. Mudgett chased after them, no longer mooing but exclaiming, "We should have gotten some popcorn! Mary Joan, I'm hunnggry! Where are you going?"

They ended up in fourth row, plopping down on plastic chairs. The screen immediately flickered and exploded with light. "Oh, this is good," Mrs. Mudgett said. "This is wonderful! A perfect view!"

The first film was in black and white, and for a moment Chris's attention was drawn above the screen where the round rafters of the barn glowed like golden ribs of a whale. Lake Superior was the backdrop for the opening credits of

Illuminating Land, the narrator explaining how the area was viewed differently by Indian tribes, French explorers, missionaries, industrialists, and the various ethnic groups that worked in the factories and mills. "And then," the narrator said, building tension while the camera flew over water and woods and hovered above a cultivated field, "there were the pioneer farmers who tried their hands at fruits and vegetables."

"That's us!" Mrs. Mudgett said. "We grow fruities and veggies!"

"Shh," Mary Joan said.

"Listen, cutie, the filmmakers are in the back row. I know some of them. They want us to show emotion for their art!"

"Shush!" someone scolded from the back row.

Mrs. Mudgett laughed and continued emoting during the entire film, making joyful noises for the old-fashioned farms and way of life; and she hummed along to the soundtrack, harmonizing with the melodies of harmonica and fiddle.

Christopher nudged Mary Joan and whispered, "This is crazy. Really awesome." He felt lost and found in a fantastical realm that seemed to exist between art and love.

Mary Joan handed him a square of chocolate. "It's semi-sweet."

"Emphasis on sweet," he replied.

The onscreen farmers suffered terribly through the years, one of them ending up with a whole century of woeful tales—blizzards, bears, wolves, floods, mosquitoes, ticks, flies, blights, pandemics, banks, and death.

"I love...this," Mrs. Mudgett said, her face drenched with tears. "I really...love it."

"Everyone is dead," the last pioneer said.

The final credits rolled while a host of harmonicas and fiddles lifted the last image—Lake Superior frozen under a great ghost of snow—skyward in a surge of light.

"Everyone lived," the last pioneer said.

Nobody in the Barn Theater seemed to know what to do. Even Mrs. Mudgett sat perfectly still, for almost five seconds. "Bravo!" she shouted, leaping to her feet, leading the audience in a standing ovation. "MOO-vie of the year! MOO-vie of the year!"

Chris stayed seated, slouched in his chair. Some folks might have thought he was embarrassed to be seen with tears on his face. But he was not embarrassed. He was simply stunned by the power of the film, and he hoped his own life would be worthy, someday, of such illumination.

Chapter Twenty-Eight

Oh, nooo.

Val Lake was pacing in the living room when Chris arrived home from the Barn. "Topher, it's almost midnight. Are you okay?"

"Hi, Mom. Yeah, the Mudgetts are lots of fun and we had a great time."

Val noticed a smudge of chocolate on her son's face. "I need to know more about these people."

"I'm visiting their farm tomorrow. I'll give you a full report."

Rubbing her throat, Val said, "I don't need a full report. Just a good synopsis."

"Okay, Mom."

Next morning, the boy rode a borrowed bicycle

(Skunk's rusty one-speed) out of the city. While he pedaled, grasshoppers played music to flowers and weeds dancing in the wind. It was a pleasant ride toward the ranches and farms, except for the hordes of horseflies air-galloping and searching for a blood feast. The boy pedaled faster to outpace the pursuers, and then slowed again, gliding for a while, not wanting to work up a stinking sweat.

The Mudgetts lived on twenty acres they called Sweet Woods. They grew a healthy variety of grains, fruits, and vegetables. They free-ranged chickens, milked goats, picked apples, made arts and crafts, and earned just enough money to continue being a family on the land.

Mary Joan watched from a window while Chris rode his bike up the gravel road to the house, but it was Mrs. Mudgett who rushed to greet him at the door. "Didn't you just love the MOO-vies last night?"

Before he could respond, Mary Joan appeared, wearing a red dress and pink scarf. "Mother, please don't moo at my guest."

"Hi Mary Joan, it's okay."

"It's not okay."

"Come in, come in," Mrs. Mudgett said. "We have the table all set. I hope you like everything goat."

"Everything goat?"

Mary Joan grabbed his arm, escorting him to the dining

room. "Don't freak out about us. Feel free to ask questions."

"Questions? Why would I have questions?"

Three people were seated at a large dinner table: a hulking father, a skinny boy, and a very pregnant girl.

Whoa, Chris thought.

The pregnant girl, seventeen, strained to stand up. "Hello, I'm Chastity."

"Yep," her twelve-year-old brother said, "and I'm Promiscuous."

Mr. Mudgett, big as a bear, growled, "Grant, you better watch yourself."

"Oh, here we go," Mary Joan said, giving Chris an apologetic glance.

"Ta-daahhh!" Mrs. Mudgett sang, point at the bewildered guest. "This is Christopher Lake, famous for going on non-dates. Isn't he a cutie?"

Nobody answered, but Chastity smiled as if saying: *Yes, the boy is a cutie.*

"Sit," Mrs. Mudgett commanded. "Let's eeeat!"

Fresh goat milk, butter, cheese, yogurt, and a covered casserole dish glistened in the sunshine pouring through the window. Grant scooped a huge glut of yogurt, plopping it on his plate, and said to the guest, "You kissed my sister yet?"

Mary Joan gave him a death glare.

"Well, excuuuse me." Grant grabbed a chunk of cheese. "I meant my other sister."

Mr. Mudgett growled loudly—to no avail—and Grant muttered, "It's not my fault my sisters are so hot."

Chastity opened the casserole dish. "Goat stew," she said, and served a large portion to Chris. "Taste it. You'll love it."

"Um, okay."

The table became silent. There was a long pause while Chris chewed the stew. Everyone stared at him to discern his honest assessment. The boy didn't show any emotion for several more seconds. And then he grinned. "Yum."

"Oh, heavens be praised!" Mrs. Mudgett's eyes began to water, and she dabbed them with a napkin. "You really, truly, sincerely—like it?"

"Yep, I do. This stew has a sweetness."

"Maple syrup," Mr. Mudgett said proudly. "I tapped it myself last winter."

Chris continued with his assessment of the stew. "I must say, this is the greatest goat I've ever tasted."

Mrs. Mudgett burst into tears. "Give him more! Give him more!"

The rest of the meal was animated by conversations ranging from organic food to music to politics to education to pure nonsense. Chris was surprised by how quickly the time passed. He helped Mary Joan with the dishes—he washed and she dried—and then everyone went outside to sit on the porch where Mrs. Mudgett made sure Chris and Mary Joan got the swing. "Oh, for cute," she said. "I should get the video camera."

"NO," Mary Joan said. "And no singing, either. I want to hear the ducks and geese."

...charged with the grandeur...

Chris contemplated the acreage, admiring the pond, garden, fields, and orchards. He asked, "How do you people survive on a farm this small?"

"We're very fertile," Grant said, glancing toward Chastity.

"Don't make me hurt you," she said, rising and wobbling toward him.

Grant leapt from the porch. "Time to check on the chickens!"

"You're a chicken yourself," Chastity said. "Bawk, bawk!"

Ignoring them, Mr. Mudgett addressed the question raised by Chris. "How do we survive out here? We put our eggs in many baskets. We sell chickens and eggs all year, turkeys during the holidays, apples and pumpkins in the fall, maple syrup in the winter, berries and veggies in the summer. We do very well at the Farmer's Market in town."

"Huh. My mom shops there."

"Does your mother buy blackberries?"

"Yeah."

"Our blackberries sell for fifteen dollars a pound. That's black gold, Christopher. Especially with free labor. You can see how often Grant gets into trouble. He works off his transgressions with extra chores."

"In forty years," Chastity said, "he might be free."

Mr. Mudgett gestured toward the land as if blessing it and receiving a blessing. "Organics. Your family eats them, Christopher. And so do many of the families in town. We survive quite well."

"We sell arts and crafts, too," Mary Joan added, quickening the swing, "especially holiday decorations—we can't keep up with demand. Mom's like a professional painter. She does nature scenes and portraits. You should see the portrait she did of my sister."

Chastity made a funny face. "Uh oh. The baby's doing back flips."

"Oh, for cute," Mrs. Mudgett said.

Chris stared at the girl's belly, looked away, and stared again. "Do you know, I mean, are you, um, never mind."

"Do I know the baby's father? Yes, of course. There's only one possibility. Are we getting married? No. Do I feel like my life is over? I've never felt more alive. Am I keeping my baby? Yes. Are my parents throwing me out of the house?"

"Don't be a silly-willy," Mrs. Mudgett said, eyes watering. "We're not thrilled with the timing, but we're thrilled with the gift."

Chapter Twenty-Nine

Summoned the next morning by a dozen tongues of birdsong, Chris arose at sunrise. He dressed in his best pants and a white linen shirt. He said a sort of prayer, had spring water for breakfast, and went outside for a walk. Or rather, a quest.

Filaments of fire sparked along the path, spider webs catching flies and light while butterflies played the sky for a mating dance. Christopher climbed the hill in thrall of all things high and low like the yellow honeysuckle at the edge of the road, their bell-shaped flowers ringing silently.

Higher up, cloud mountains appeared, suggesting kingdom upon kingdom, and Chris imagined castles and dragons and—

Greep. Greep!

A gleaming flycatcher, perched in a pine, proudly displayed a prize in its beak—a snakeskin.

Chris laughed. "Let it go, bird. Let it go."

Greep. Greep! The bird flew away, snakeskin writhing in the wind.

What would Father Hopkins say about that?

Chris marched to the top of the hill, his breathing easy, legs untired. Near a stone building, he turned and looked down at the harbor with its ominous luminosity arising though mist. The great lake was beckoning as if claiming the beauty of a church.

Chris was, in fact, at the steps of a church.

"Welcome, welcome," the greeters said, two elderly ladies with sweet smiles.

The boy turned and faced the door. "Is it time?"

The lovely ladies harmonized, "Come in. Come in."

Well, look at that!

The Mudgetts were there in the front row. *I thought they didn't like preaching.*

Chris crept into a back pew and tried his best to follow along with the liturgy. He stood when everyone else stood, sat when they sat, kneeled when they kneeled, and knew enough to stay out of the Communion line. Actually, he was too enthralled to move, barely able to breathe. By some trick of stained glass or sunlight mixed with candlelight,

Chris saw sparks and smoke rising from the chalice. And when Mary Joan received the Holy Gifts, her whole body turned into flame.

Chapter Thirty

Moosehead bellowed into the phone, "Join our team! Business is really booming! C'mon. Mow lawns with us."

"Hmm."

"Skunk and I are getting rich! Filthy rich!"

"Really?"

"Um, no, not really. But we're making decent coin—and getting filthy."

Chris had been mowing his parents' lawn for a pittance. He was a competent mower, able to make straight lines, and he knew the difference between grass and gardens. So why not join a business venture and earn some wealth?

"Sure. Count me in."

"Cool, dude! It'll be awesome!"

It was lawn-mowing hell. Moosehead and Skunk gave

Chris the worst job in town, a lawn with inclines that would challenge a mountain goat to jump to its death. The mower Chris pushed was not self-propelling, so he had to strain up and down the dangerous hills to earn his meager pay. He cursed Sisyphus—the name he gave to the mower—and became so frustrated that he simply killed the engine. He sat beneath an oak, resting in the shade, listening to the landscape.

Chris knew that wherever there were trees, there was music: cicada soloists; chipmunks chanting jazz; doves cooing and wooing; and birds of every rhythmic wing adding their universal notes. The boy could have listened all day, but there was work to be done, money to make. So he fired up Sisyphus, killing the music, filling the hillside with more exhaust.

He took Sunday off. Waking from a dream that ended with a dead dragon, he crawled out of bed, sore as heck, got dressed in his best, then went outside and disappeared into a great cloud that had descended upon the city. From Mount Royal down to the shore of Superior, the cloud hovered over everything as if laying claim. Christopher searched for the veiled sun, found a faint glow, and couldn't stop staring. Words came to mind like an ancient music he refused to forget and refused to re-accept: *And so, humbly trust the blind stirring of love in your heart. Not your physical heart, your will.*

He had a glimpse of Terra for a moment, sadly shook it away, then limped slowly through the cloud up to Holy Spirit. Arriving to Mass late, he slunk into the back row while Father Karl was telling a joke. "Sven and Ole went to Rome to ask the Pope if he approved of Catholics gambling. And the Pope proclaimed: You betcha!"

Silence.

"Get it? You bet...cha."

A few people laughed, including Mrs. Mudgett who guffawed graciously, knowing the difficulty of entertaining a captive audience. "Bravo, Father! Bravo!"

Oh, no.

Grant slid beside Chris in the back row. "Got a smoke, homie?"

"Shh. Shouldn't you be in the front with your family?"

"I've been hiding out in the bathroom. Can I sit with you?"

"Not unless you behave."

"You sound like my dad."

"You sound like a bad kid."

"Listen," Grant said, looking Chris in the eye, "we're all good Catholics here. You're the one who's the heathen."

Chapter Thirty-One

Grant Mudgett was a hellion in most situations. But when doing farm work, he could be a saint. The boy performed many chores—milking goats, gathering eggs, watering the garden—happily finding his vocation in such things, especially on summer days that sang of Eden.

"You've never milked a goat?"

"Nope," Chris said.

"You're kidding. Who hasn't milked a goat?"

"Show me how."

"Fine. Prepare to be amazed." Grant fastened the goat securely, positioned himself on a stool, and reached out for Miss America. "Just grab her like this. You don't wanna pull. It's more of a squeeze. Very gently."

Miss America raised a hoof to kick Grant in the head.

"Careful," Chris warned, moving away, "she's about to—"

"Yee haw! Let there be milk!"

"Well, look at that. Good work."

The bucket began filling, and Mary Joan appeared, wearing a golden sun dress. *Wow.* Chris could hardly keep from staring, forcing himself to point at the milk bucket. "Your brother is quite the farmer."

"Yes, quite."

"Your family's very fortunate," Chris said. "If the grocery stores ever close down, you'll be saved."

"Saved. Yes. It's good to be saved. "Mary Joan smiled and gently petted Miss America. "Good girl, good girl."

"Last Sunday," Chris said, "Father Karl sent all goats to Hell."

"What? No, he didn't."

"Yes, he did. Father Karl said sheep will enter Heaven. And goats gonna burn."

"Don't be silly," Mary Joan said, shaking her head. "You have to know what's symbolic and what's real."

Leaning over, Chris tried to give her a quick little kiss—to prove that he knew what was real—but the girl turned and walked away, not saying a word.

"Gross," Grant said. "That kiss would've been gross."

Chapter Thirty-Two

The next Sunday was another sweet Sabbath, and after sitting with the Mudgetts in the front pew at Mass, Chris was invited to the farm for goat stew, goat milk, goat cheese, and goat yogurt with fresh, organic strawberries. And goat chocolate.

After the feast, the Mudgetts wanted to play a parlor game called "Word Face" in which a person picks a word from a hat and tries to make a face to match that word. The other players then guess the word being expressed. Mr. Mudgett went first, picking the word "joy." He made some earnest faces, but nobody was able to guess correctly. After a few minutes, he growled and gave up. "Joy," he said. "I thought it was obvious."

His wife teased him. "You call that joy? Those serious

faces? That's not joy!"

"It was joy enough," he replied.

Mary Joan went next. She was a great player at Word Face, able to express the unique intricacies of a human, immortal soul.

"Agony!" Chris guessed.

"Dang," she said, showing the word on paper. "You guessed it instantly. You're so attuned."

"I'm outta here," Grant said, heading for the door. "I'm attuned to shoveling manure."

"Myy turrrn! Myy turrrn!" Mrs. Mudgett, with all her wondrous enthusiasm and acting experience, was no good at the game, exaggerating each emotion to the point of making it silly.

The girls loved it, especially Chastity. "Flighty? Your word was flighty? Mom, that was insanity!"

"I was perfectly flighty, and you know it."

"Haha."

"Tee hee."

Chris won, followed by Mary Joan. Then it was time for "Words, Words, Words," another game that made everyone laugh. Mr. Mudgett wouldn't play that one. Instead, he leaned back in his chair and whittled a chunk of wood, carving a small bear to sell at the Farmer's Market.

"Here wee gooo," Mrs. Mudgett sang. "Christopher

shall give us a good word! C'mon, now, make it really good."

"Um, okay." Chris thought up a great word: *date*. And he gave the clue. "A boy and girl go on a..."

The answer was given instantaneously.

"Cruise!" the women all shouted.

Chris shook his head and tried again. "When a boy likes a girl, they go on a..."

"Cruise!" the women shouted.

"No, that's not it. A boy will ask a girl to go out...on a..."

"Cruise!"

The timer went off. "Sorry," the boy said. "It was a date."

Chastity laughed. "Exactly. A cruise."

"Hey, I have a great idea," Mrs. Mudgett said, her brain happily buzzing on goat chocolate. "Christopher, why don't you take Mary Joan on a cruise?"

"What?" Mr. Mudgett nicked himself with the knife. "I don't think—"

"The Friday cruise is the best," Chastity said. "Duluth from the harbor is so beautiful. Oh, you will love it."

Mary Joan's eyes dared the boy to take her on a harbor cruise. He nodded an affirmative, followed by a nervous pause.

The nervous pause was caused, of course, by Mr. Mudgett. The old growler was whittling again, finger bleeding on the bear. After an eternal minute, he said, "Mary Joan's not allowed to date." He lifted the knife and pointed it at the boy. "Never."

"Oh, it's not a date," Chastity said. "It's only sightseeing. It's educational. And besides, they'll be surrounded by a boat-load of chaperones. Most of them will be old fuddy-duddies who live to spy and snoop."

"Oh, for cute," Mrs. Mudgett said, nodding enthusiastically. "I approve of this."

"Okay," Christopher said, grinning at Mary Joan. "Friday night it is."

"Friday night it is," she replied. "It will be a lovely non-date."

Chastity and her mother burst out with "Whoo-hoo!" And they followed that with clapping, high fives, and a "Whoo-eee!"

"I had no chance," Mr. Mudgett muttered to the bear.

Chapter Thirty-Three

Shrouded in mist, Mrs. Mudgett waved goodbye to the ship, barely able to see the kids floating away. "Be good! Have fun! Don't go overboard! Marryy Jooan, do you have your phoone?"

"I have my phone," she replied. "I'll be sure to call if we sink."

"Okay, I'll be back in an hour to pick you up! *Bon voyage!* That means good voyage!"

"Right, Mom. Bye."

Alone at last, Chris thought. *Well, sort of alone.*

They'd boarded with about fifty other people. Most of the cruisers seemed local, or tourists who were true fans of Minnesota, wearing sweatshirts that pledged allegiance to the Vikings, Twins, Gophers, or Wild. The ship's horn wailed through the fog as the Vista King slowly chugged through the inlet toward deep water.

"We are really cruising now," a disembodied voice said, beginning to narrate the voyage. "Look westward and behold the city on a hill."

Chris looked, saw only a cloud, and had to imagine what was above the harbor: humble, weather-beaten homes perched on cliffs with mansions and churches, all hinting of heavenly architecture.

"Oh, wow." Mary Joan pointed at another part of the sky. "Look at that."

The sun was breaking through, creating a column of solid light.

"And look down there," Chris said.

The column had formed a circle in the water, widening and intensifying.

"Perfect," Mary Joan said. "It's a perfect day."

While the ship chugged along, the narrator intoned facts and figures about Lake Superior, including that it reaches "the almost unfathomable depth of a thousand feet down."

A pair of loons surfaced in the circle of light, laughing.

"Oh, I love the loons." Mary Joan kissed her non-date on the cheek. "I love this."

Note to self, the boy thought: *cruise, cruise, cruise!*

"Superior is a great graveyard," the narrator said.

"Buried in these waters are three-hundred and fifty ships."

A guy in Vikings gear smirked. "Fifteen more wrecks and we'll have one for every day of the year. A whole calendar of destruction. Skoal!"

The narrator continued. "Wind gusts can reach seventy miles per hour in the relative safety of the harbor—with waves reaching thirty feet. The lift bridge must rise to allow the giant waves to pass through."

The ship ventured further out. A screeching gull swooped down and checked the deck for food. A puff of popcorn pleased the scavenger, and it screeched again. The guy in Vikings gear tried to kick-box the gull, missed, and fell on his butt. Several people snickered, and someone in a Packers jersey whispered, "Karma."

The narrator intoned, "This concludes the deep-water part of the cruise. Now we will turn the ship around and give you an in-depth tour of the dock yards and storage facilities."

Several people groaned and complained about how fast the "good part of the cruise" had ended.

Chris agreed with them. "A boy and girl...go on a... cruise. And don't want to see a grain elevator."

"Yes they do," Mary Joan said. "Don't you want to learn about grain elevators?"

Chugging along, the ship entered the maze of industry,

with Chris complaining, "It's ugly as hell."

Rust, peeling paint, mottled cement walls, piles of nondescript debris, mounds of scrap metal, oily rocks, gravel, coal, heaps and heaps of garbage. The boy began to feel nauseous.

Mary Joan frowned. "Why is the shipyard like this? I mean, we do a lot of work on our farm. And our farm stays beautiful."

"I know." Chris gently put an arm around her, his stomach churning. "I know why your farm is beautiful."

"Why?"

"You, of course."

The girl awaited his next move, assuming more charm, more than a kiss on the cheek.

The boy puckered—as the ship faltered—and he lurched at Mary Joan's face, slobbering the worst possible kiss all over her mouth. He may have thrown up a little, and that was just too much. That was the end of the cruise and the end of the romance.

Chapter Thirty-Four

Moosehead called a few weeks later, bellowing into the phone, “Sacramento! You’re a lucky dude!”

“Oh,” Chris said, staring out a window, contemplating the Ruins. “How am I lucky?”

“The groundskeeper at the nursing home lost his toe! He can’t work right now. So you get to replace him.”

“Why can’t you or Skunk replace him?”

Skunk took control of the phone. “We-we messed up already.”

“You lost your toes, too?”

“We-we sort of crashed the tractor.”

“Sort of crashed it?” Chris imagined the scene. “The two of you were driving the tractor at the same time, fighting over the wheel.”

"Yeah, and we-we sort of crashed. And we-we got fired."

Taking the phone back, Moosehead explained, "We're horrible, but you're dependable! You won't get fired the first day."

"I already mow some lawns. Why would I want this job?"

"Because it pays better. And you get to ride a tractor—if they ever fix it."

"Hmm."

"It's all resting on you, Sacramento. We promised to provide someone dependable to make up for us. Because we're horrible."

"I don't know, guys. I'm not feeling inspired. I'm gonna say no."

Skunk yelled into the phone, "We-we saw a woods by the nursing home—with a nice pond! You can take breaks there and smoke-smoke!"

"I don't smoke."

Moosehead tried to be logical. "Then don't smoke! Crap! But listen, the nursing home is a deal of a lifetime. And it's being offered to you, free of charge."

Chris paused for a few moments, thinking he should hang up; and he burst out laughing. The semi-gracious absurdity of his friends was exactly what he needed to ease his heartbreak. "Okay, fine. I'll go to the nursing home and see if they'll hire me."

They did. Full-time, with overtime pay. From sunrise until sunset, Chris drove a brand-new tractor to tame and beautify the earth. At first, he drove the tractor very slowly, dependably, eyes straight ahead, but after a week or so, his lines became crooked because he got distracted by the sky.

As kingfishers catch fire...

He almost crashed several times.

Chapter Thirty-Five

Sunburned and wind-kissed, Chris liked to sleep with the window open, sleeping very soundly, but one sultry midnight found him still awake, the turning constellations burning something in his soul. He got out of bed, kneeling and shivering on the floor, wanting to pray in a new way, or the original way, words resounding with the Ancient of Days; but he felt blocked, his tongue unable to make such talk that would properly honor the Word. He knelt in silence for a good hour, not sure if that counted as praying, not sure if he was worthy of approaching Unapproachable Light, not sure if he was awake or dreaming this latest quest; and then he felt a jolt—not quite a lightning bolt—and felt inspired to remember words that were not his, and yet were kindred spirits of his words.

Under the bed was a box of books.

"I remember." Still kneeling, he opened the box and perused the star-lit tomes, his attention lingering upon *Visions of the Medieval Mystics*. "Gift from Professor Corwin."

Chris had tried many times to forget about the Corwins and the cathedral, library, and mysterious upper room. His heart began pounding, as if never before, and the boy held the book to his heart. *Give her a call.*

Okay, but Terra had no cell phone, as far as he knew, so he'd have to call the land line. And what would happen if Mrs. Corwin answered the midnight ring? Would she scold him with a voice colder than Lake Superior? If Terra didn't pick up the phone, he hoped it would be the professor. Chris would say, "Silvenshine! Silvenshine! May I please converse with your lovely granddaughter?"

Christopher dropped the book into the box, picked up his phone, and dialed the cathedral. His adrenaline doubled from the first ring to the second, and by the third and fourth rings, he was certain he would die of the most massive heart attack in human history. After the fifth ring, he decided to hang up and save his life; but he held on for one more.

"Hello?"

Such a beautiful, song-like voice. How could he ever

forget it?

It was Mary Joan Mudgett. He'd dialed the wrong number.

"Um," the boy said.

"Chris?"

"Yeah. It's me. Hey, Mary Joan."

"You know how late it is?"

"Sorry. I couldn't sleep."

She yawned loudly. "You know, I couldn't sleep either. It's such a perfect night. The stars. Did you see the stars?"

"Yeah, the stars are awesome."

"Can you hear the baby crying?"

"The baby? Oh, Chastity! That's right. Did she have a girl?"

"A boy. Joseph."

"A great name."

"Yes. One of the best."

"Um, well, say hi from me to them. And to all your family. And you, Mary Joan—"

"Me? What about me?"

The boy stared out the window, feeling at a loss in that wilderness of light. "I, um, want to apologize. I hope we can be friends again. And...and...are you going to East High this year?"

"No, I'm doing home school. So I can help Chastity with the baby."

"Oh. That's good of you."

"Chastity would do the same for me."

The image of Mary Joan pregnant made the boy blush, and he felt a rush of guilt. "Well, I should let you get your sleep."

The girl paused, making him wonder if she'd say something punishing. After a few moments, she said, "I miss you. Will you be at Mass on Sunday?"

"No, I have to mow."

"You have to moo?"

"Mow."

"On the Sabbath? You can't take off one hour?"

"Moosehead and Skunk are counting on me. I don't want to let them down."

"I've never understood you, Christopher."

"Me either," he said, turning from the window. "Sorry, I should have told you right away. I dialed the wrong number. I was meaning to call—"

Click.

She hung up on him.

Chapter Thirty-Six

"Dang," Chris muttered on Sunday morning, "look at that fog. The grass will be wet."

Wet grass meant he'd have to double-mow some sections and rake extra debris. He hated raking. "I won't do it. Nope. Not raking today. Just not gonna. Just not."

Instead, he decided to sit by the nursing-home pond and wait for the sun to shine. "Ahh," this is good." He reclined on a dry patch beneath an oak canopy and waited for the world to brighten.

It darkened. A hard rain began to fall, finding its way through the canopy and blessing the boy's ungrateful face. He stood and cursed, felt instantly guilty, than found himself staring at a leaf, one of a million and yet unique, uplifted like a small, green grail. Chris gave thanks without even thinking about it, and witnessed a hummingbird drink from the cup. The sky poured and poured, the wings disappeared, and Chris watched the pond lighting up with tiny splashes as if thousands of hummingbirds were diving in and flittering up again. And then the heavens burst with thunder as the sun reappeared with a sun shower, everything bright and silver and golden.

"Good God..."

Chapter Thirty-Seven

In the fall, Chris met a student at East who wanted to become a priest. Trevor Nelson wore thick glasses and between classes squinted at a shiny poster in his locker, an image of Christ in a sky full of hovering letters like birds born of calligraphy:

I AM
THE RESURRECTION
AND THE LIFE

Chris wanted Trevor to know he appreciated the sign of hope, so he slapped the kid on the back. "Cool pic!" Chris didn't know his own strength and sent the thick glasses falling, shattering.

"Sorry! I didn't mean to—"

Trevor fell to his knees, trying to gather the fragments.

"These lenses were supposed to be shatter-proof. My dad paid extra. Oh, man, I'm in trouble."

"I'm really sorry," Chris said, kneeling to help clean up the mess.

"No, it's okay. Anyway, it must be God's will."

"Are you sure? God wanted me to break your glasses?"

"Go to class, brother. Don't be late because of me."

Christopher stood. "You sure?"

"I'm sure," Trevor said, his hands sweeping the brokenness into a pile.

Twenty minutes later, Chris was sitting in art class, gazing out the window at the sky, when the teacher began speaking in an almost secretive rasp. "Surrender to your intuition how the white light and black light, rayon blanc and rayon noir, collect together in the same droplet of paint—and make something like blood. Imagine that. And re-imagine that. Um, excuse me. Mr. Daydreamer? Do you want to learn about art? Or not?"

"Oh, yeah," Chris said. "It's beautiful."

"Art sucks," a kid slurred. The kid was a tobacco chewer named Duane Schmidt. All day long, Duane drooled boggish liquid into a Coke can.

The teacher ignored him. "Absorb into your deepest appreciation how Monet's water lilies reveal the veiled life within the liquid spirit of the pond."

Spit! "I don't see life in that pond. Where's the tadpoles? Where's the leeches?"

"Water represents the soul—perhaps the soul of the artist, or maybe the soul of the viewer—and even obscured by this too, too solid flesh, it can be a wonder of colorful symmetry in harmony with the All."

Spit!

After class, in the hallway chaos, Chris ended up walking next to the tobacco chewer and he tried to be polite. "Strange lecture, right?"

"Worthless. No leeches in any paintings."

"Well, class will improve when we do our own paintings, eh Dip?"

"What did you call me?"

"Dip. That's what everyone calls you."

Duane smiled vengefully. "See you around, dipshit."

After school, Chris meandered by the football field on his way to the nursing home. Despite how muscular and athletic he'd become, and despite an invitation from the coach to try out for the team, he'd decided he'd rather make money than suffer concussions.

The after-school light dimmed and chilled as the September days passed, and at the end of the month Chris was told that the nursing home no longer needed his services. The regular groundskeeper had returned with a reattached toe.

For Christ plays in ten thousand places...Lovely in limbs...

The boy found work raking leaves for his neighbors (not quite loving it) and in the winter he shoveled snow (hating it) and before dinner he got in the habit of climbing Mount Royal to get a drink. Taking no heed of his mother's warnings, Chris had become addicted to "the bad magic bean." He bought the boldest brew at Caribou Coffee, asked for a mug instead of a cup, and sipped the elixir by the fireplace. While contemplating dancing light, he couldn't help but overhear conversations, and he became intrigued by the epic tales of typical Minnesotans, their stories full of romance, pain, suffering, and sometimes redemption.

Inspired, he began scribbling verses on napkins.

A woman by the frozen window lives in a memory
of a dream buried by an enemy
now a friend of winter's dead.
And she tells the story to bring him back—alive again.

The old woman by the frozen window took notice of the young writer, and asked him, "Do you go to Cathedral High School?"

The boy shook his head. "East."

She gave him a maternal smile. "Are you a senior?"

Chris laughed. "Ninth grade."

"Oh my. You seem so mature."

"I'm fifteen," he said, crumpling up the poem. "Just a freshman."

"Well," the old woman said, eyes watering. "Enjoy your life, fresh man."

He tossed the crumpled napkin into the fire. "Okay. I'll try."

Chapter Thirty-Eight

Blessings upon curses, the next summer Chris was pushing Sisyphus again, battling unruly yards up and down the slopes, his muscles exploding with power. He was sweating profusely, partly because of the westerly wind uncooled by the lake, and partly because he'd let his hair grow long and thick. His parents didn't like the wild locks, but what could ex-hippies say? His mom said, "Uncontrolled follicles are a leading cause of endocrine sickness."

"Haha," the young man answered. "Just call me Samson."

One afternoon in a yard nearest the Ruins, Chris was mowing furiously—his strength and speed in perfect coordination—when a red pickup appeared. Chris felt like the truck didn't belong there, and he paused to see who would get out.

It was a gum-chomping man wearing an East High T-shirt and a buzz-cut. It was the football coach. "Hey, kid! Yeah, you!"

Chris killed the mower. "Um, you need a lawn mowed?"

"Nope. I need a running back." The coach chomped his gum as if trying to kill it. "People been talking about you."

"Talking about me?"

Chomp, chomp. "You Lake?"

"Yeah. I'm Christopher."

The coach nodded. "See you on the field in the fall."

"Hmm. Maybe."

Chomp, chomp. "Keep mowing this summer, lift weights, run sprints every day. I think you can make the team. Even be a starter."

"Really? Well, huh. Okay."

"And get a damn haircut. And stay away from girls."

Chapter Thirty-Nine

Pixie Johnson, cheerleader extraordinaire, soared in the air as if the cosmos had been especially created for her. Chris could hear Pixie's spiraling voice while he mastered the field, bashing his body against the other Friday-night warriors. Distracted whenever the redhaired wonder leapt heavenward, he wanted to run and catch her. And keep her.

"Keep your focus, Lake!" the coach yelled. "Focus!"

Pixie wore a body-kissing black leotard and shouted, "Go Christopher! Kill 'em!"

Chris was a natural, knowing when to accelerate, pivot, cut back, redirect, and lower his head into the guts of defenders, smashing his way into the end zone.

"Christopher! Christopher!"

Pixie cheered louder than the other girls, as if making a claim.

Glancing at her with a grin, the boy was in bliss to be involved in such endeavors. He'd never before considered sports as a good way to spend time on earth, especially football with its brutal injuries. But when he was given the ball on the battlefield, something beyond the prospect of injury arose in his soul. It was like an instinct or a calling, a need to conquer for a cause, and he gained a hundred yards and scored two touchdowns in his first game.

Pixie approached him afterwards. "You're amazing. Really amazing."

He grinned. "You are."

"Thanks. Um, see you around." And Pixie flew away with her friends.

The following Monday, he saw her in the cafeteria. "Hey," he said, "we should meet at Caribou after practice."

Mulling over the offer, Pixie played with her hair and replied in a flirty voice, "You and me? And coffee? Oh, no thanks."

The answer hit his chest and almost knocked the wind out of him. Chris wasn't sure how to pivot or redirect the conversation to avoid further injury. "I think," he said, trying to think, "that maybe, um, maybe—"

"We should skip the coffee shop," Pixie said. "Just

come over to my house after supper." She paused, acting all innocent. "We'll watch old episodes of *Little House on the Prairie*."

"*Little House on the Prairie?*"

"Yeah. With my mom."

That didn't seem like the perfect date, but Chris said, "Okay. Sounds good."

The Johnson family lived in a tough neighborhood with no view of the lake. The ramshackle abode was hot in summer and cold in winter and almost crumbled when airplanes from the military base roared over. Pixie's father was a failed pilot who'd fallen into a dead-end job at the paper mill. Her mother had been a beauty princess, but never a queen, a runner-up several times. She ended up going to beauty school to become a stylist.

Pixie and Chris watched *Little House on the Prairie* on a beer-stained couch with drunken Mrs. Johnson. She slurred at her daughter. "Your friend is cute. I like his long hair. Brown and curly. Oo la la."

"Mom, watch the TV."

"He dresses nice, too. White linen shirt. Gotta love a boy that wears natural fibers."

"Mom."

"Almost no wrinkles on that shirt. I'll bet he knows how to iron. Oo la la."

Mrs. Johnson munched peanut brittle and gulped beer. During the commercials, she offered brittle to the football player.

"No thanks," Chris said. "But, um, thanks."

"You sure?"

"I had a big supper."

"Your mom make steak?"

"Cauliflower casserole. Raw."

"Yuckie poo. Here, have a snack."

"I'm not hungry. Really. We also had bean-sprout salad."

"Oh my gosh!" Mrs. Johnson spewed brittle in disbelief. "Oh my heck!"

It was the episode where little Carrie falls down a mine. It was nearly as good, on a romantic level, as a horror movie, because Pixie nervously leaned on Chris's shoulder and held his arm.

If only we were alone, he thought, *if only...*

Mrs. Johnson gulped more beer. "Oh, thank you, Lord! Little Carrie's alive! She needs a bath, that's for sure, but she's okay." *Burp.* She turned off the TV and staggered down the hallway to the bedroom, leaving the teenagers alone on the couch.

Pixie wiped a tear and buried another into the boy's shoulder. "I'm sorry," she said. "Maybe it was a mistake to invite you here."

"No. I'm glad to be here. With you." Chris gently stroked her hair. "It's awesome. I mean, you're awesome." She turned her face to his, and they kissed. And kissed again.

This is the life, the boy thought, *this is the life*. "Pixie," he said, sighing heavily.

The cheerleader waited for him to catch his breath. "Chris. Can I ask you a question? It's fairly serious."

"Um, okay," he said, "if that's what you want to do now."

"Do you ever think about your soul?"

"My soul?"

"Yeah," the girl said. "I think about my soul all the time. I feel like it wants to fly away."

"Now? You're thinking that now?"

Pixie stared innocently into his ravenous eyes. "Do you believe in things? Things that really matter? Do you believe in soul-mates?"

"Um. What?"

"Soul-mates."

"Well, um," he said, pointing at the window. "What's that?"

A flash of light hit the glass, stronger than moonlight—a car pulling into the driveway. "My dad's home," she said nervously. "Go sit in that chair."

"What chair?"

"On the other side of the room. Hurry!"

A downstairs door opened and closed. Footsteps shuffled, and a whiskey voice called out, "What the hell's this? Lorraine! Where are you? This place is a sty." Mr. Johnson stomped up the stairs, swearing every few steps, and found his wife passed out in the bedroom. "Wake the hell up, Lorraine."

"Chris," Pixie whispered. "You should probably run."

"No," he said, knowing this wasn't a game. "I should stay here with you."

One room away, Mr. Johnson kicked the bed. "Lorraine! Wake the hell up!"

"Oh, Gus, Gussy. Careful, walls cave in."

"What walls?"

"In the pit—she fell."

"Pixie? What happened? What pit?"

"Don't be a dumbshit, Gus. That old mine—swallowed her up."

"She home? Or out wreckin' her life again?"

"She's home. Good family time."

"Yer drunk."

"Yer drunker."

"Any beer in the fridge?"

"Down a pit. Down a pit. So good."

"Where the hell's Pixie?"

"TV room."

"She didn't sneak out?"

"Nope."

"She's watchin' TV?"

"Don't be silly. *Little House* ended. It was horrible."

Gus raised his voice to be heard in the whole house. "Is Pixie ALONE?"

The girl motioned for Chris to sneak down the stairs. He shook his head. He'd fight Gus if he had to, or at least tackle him. That would be the right move, right? Chris really wanted to make all the right moves.

The cheerleader whispered, "Go. Now!"

Almost falling, Christopher slunk down the stairs, while Pixie called out, "Hi Daddy! Yeah, I'm all alone. Totally alone."

Chapter Forty

Near the football field, a golden leaf fell from an ancient elm, got caught in a gust of wind, and returned to the sky like a bird.

Chris tried to focus on practice, but his soul was troubled and distracted. When the quarterback handed him the ball, Chris fumbled. He tried to scoop it up, but the ball bounced away. The star running back tripped over his own feet, fell on his back, and lay motionless, staring at the golden leaf hovering above him.

"Idiot!" the coach yelled. "Get up!"

Christopher stayed on the ground, watching the goldenness disappear into a darkening sky, a thundering sky, with a storm rolling in from the lake. Whistles blew, voices commanded, and football practice was ended by larger forces. A flash of lightning burned through the air, branching in all directions as if searching for flesh.

"Christopher!" the coach yelled. "Get the hell up! Move it! I don't want a lawsuit because of you!"

The star stayed motionless, the beginning of a poem surging in his soul:

In the beginning was the kiss...and the kiss was fire...and the fire was...

Chapter Forty-One

A yellow Beetle was Chris's first car, and he named it Majestic. On a bright fall Sunday, he exchanged four-hundred dollars for the old rustbucket and drove it home, backfiring and sparking all the way.

"You need to pay for your own insurance," his father said, standing in the driveway. "And gas doesn't grow on trees."

"Yeah, I'll rake more leaves."

"And you'll need to shovel more snow."

"I will."

"Will you? What if it doesn't snow?"

Chris laughed, "No snow in Duluth? Then I'll sell suntan lotion."

Val appeared from the house, jumping up and down, her pink sari billowing. "What a sweet Beetle! So sweet!

Let's go for a ride!" She reached for the passenger-side door and was stopped by her husband's words.

"We should let him go—alone."

"Aww, it's such a fun little car. Topher, sweetie, you'll take me for a ride later?"

"Of course."

"Stay within the city limits," Joe said. "And remember what you learned in driver's ed."

"Okay, I will."

Chris flew away, grinding the gears. *Far out*, he thought, trying to see everything ahead, behind, to the sides, and above. He ascended the hill to Skyline Drive, where a hawk whirled higher in the wind, wings full of physics and metaphysics.

"Yikes!"

With a swerve in time, he avoided plunging over a cliff.

"Driver's ed," he told himself, "remember driver's ed."

Slowing for a while, then picking up speed again, Chris drove Majestic to Mount Royal, honking at the library and Caribou Coffee, and then lighting out for the farms. The land above Duluth reminded him of the landscape of Sacramento, the same striving of the trees to reach the clouds, the artistic tangling of the earthbound to be fully arisen.

"Why—why—am I here?" he muttered, realizing he'd driven out to the Mudgett farm. He shifted into neutral and coasted quietly, hoping he wouldn't be noticed.

The Mudgetts were gathered on their porch, all except for Grant who was in the yard. Grant leaned forward like a long jumper, preparing to leap into a mountain of fire-colored leaves. Christopher could see—in a rush of seconds—Mrs. Mudgett singing, her husband whittling, Chastity nursing the baby, and, in a golden dress, Mary Joan, just being beautiful.

Grant disappeared into the leaves while Chris rolled past. Nobody seemed to notice the Beetle, except for a few roaming chickens and the goat. Miss America stared as if she recognized the blushing driver and wanted him to stop.

Christopher shifted and sped away, hoping the Mudgetts were well but thinking he'd never visit their road again. He clicked on the radio, found a Golden Oldies station, and nodded to the rhythm of *The Wanderer*, winding his way around more farms and fallow fields until there was nothing but woods. He knew his parents were anxiously waiting for him at the house—his father wanting to discuss expenses and his mother wanting a ride—so it was selfish to continue this quest.

"Just a little further," he said, and repeated it several times, taking random roads through the wilderness. He didn't know where he was, but he didn't feel lost, thinking he'd eventually dead-end at the lake. And from there, finding home would be easy. The radio played Doris Day, Dean Martin, Buddy Holly, Judy Garland, and Elvis. Chris sang some lyrics about the warnings of wise men and how fools rush in. And a sign appeared.

TWO HARBORS.

Two Harbors!

"Okay, okay..." Waves of adrenaline pounded his heart as he considered driving to the cathedral.

Should I? Should I?

No. Absolutely not.

Why not?

Why not?

Yes, he would show up out of the blue at the Gothic mansion, stride up to the great door and ring the bell; and no matter who answered, he'd make a grand proclamation about his eternal feelings for Terra. What those feelings were, exactly, Chris didn't know, but the word love seemed likely to be uttered...*yes, the word love... the word love...maybe*...and he panicked and slammed on the brakes—forgetting driver's ed—and Majestic skidded across the center line into the lane of oncoming traffic.

God! What am I doing?

Checking his mirrors, downshifting, he turned Majestic around and into the right lane, barely avoiding a beer truck that would have smashed him dead, while

Dylan's voice began scratching out of the dash—
Knockin' on Heaven's Door.

Chapter Forty-Two

Pixie gave Chris a call, her uplifting voice the first message on his new phone. "Hey," she said, "ever been to Sunshine Laundromat? Haha. What a question, right? Anyway, it's maybe the best place in all of Duluth. They have an aviary—a bird sanctuary—above the machines, so people can wash their clothes while tropical feathers flutter around. It's awesome, totally awesome. Whoever thought of putting birds and laundry together is a genius. I'm there now. Call me."

Chris got the message a few minutes later and drove through a cloud of fog to see Pixie at Sunshine.

"Hey," she said, "you and your wheels found me."

"Yeah. How you doing, Pix? How is—"

She smiled beyond her suffering. "Can't complain.

Not today."

"Okay," he said, giving her hug. He wanted to kiss her, of course, and yet held back, unsure where things were at.

The two friends reclined in old stuffed chairs and watched the tropical birds at play.

"Totally amazing," Pixie said. "All that color. It's like we're not even in Duluth."

"Oh, we're in Duluth," Chris said, pointing at the mist swirling outside the window.

Pixie didn't look outside. Instead, she checked the machines to see if her cheerleading outfit and other clothes were dry. "Not yet," she said sadly. "And the minutes are all gone. Seriously? This isn't fair. This is a—"

Before she could finish the sentence, Chris plunked some quarters into the machines. "My treat," he said.

"Oh, thanks." She give him a little kiss on the cheek. "That's really nice of you."

"It's just a few quarters. Cheaper than buying dinner and a movie."

"Oh, you're so romantic."

"I am?"

She shook her head. "Not really. I mean, well, you have your moments."

"Is that why you like me? For my romantic moments?"

The girl smiled and played with her hair and gave him a

flirty look, a very flirty look.

Or was it angelical?

Chapter Forty-Three

Coach Lundblat chomped his gum and yelled, "Call a damn play that works!"

The offensive coordinator, Mr. Heitilla, sent the signal to the quarterback. "Thirty-three power." That was a tailback play for Christopher to find light between the left guard and tackle. Shifting through the line of scrimmage, leaving defenders grasping for air, Chris whirled down the field and into the end zone.

Pixie leaped and cheered, her voice rising over the crowd that included college scouts scribbling enthusiastic notes about the sophomore sensation, the God-gifted kid who'd never played football before in his life.

#30 politely tossed the ball to the stunned ref who spit out his whistle in disbelief. He'd never seen a kid so easily score a touchdown.

Knocking on Heaven's Door rasped from the dash after the game while Chris and Pixie were parking on Skyline Drive. The temperature had been dropping all night and steam between kisses began fogging the windshield, blocking starlight. Occasionally, a car careened around the bend and flashed its brights through misted glass, the diffusion making soft haloes around the boy and girl.

"Stop, stop," Pixie said.

The boy had just been cheered by a whole stadium for not stopping, so the command made no sense to his flesh. Pixie leaned away and rolled down the passenger-side window, letting in the October chill along with a swath of burning sky.

"Christopher."

"Yeah?"

"Do you ever want to leave?"

"Leave what?"

Pixie sighed and craned her neck toward the stars. "I wanna go someplace like Sunshine."

"Laundry? Now?"

"Augh. You don't understand."

He whispered, "That's for sure."

She eyed a favorite constellation. "I'd like to live someplace far away—with tropical birds all around. Like

Rio de Janeiro. Or Belize."

"So far away? You could at least stay in the country. Florida has flamingoes."

"Florida?" Pixie shook her head. "No, I'm not big on flamingoes. I like small birds, darting birds, you know, those quick flashes of color. I could watch those birds all day and night. Yeah. Let's go to the laundromat."

"Symbolically? Or for real?"

"Don't be a goof. I always talk for real."

You have got to be kidding me. She wants to go to the laundromat. At his moment...

Chris revved the engine, much louder than was necessary, and drove Majestic around the dangerous curves of Skyline and down the hill while Pixie talked more about wanting to leave town. "Chris, don't you think Duluth is plain and boring?"

"Nope. Nope I don't," he said, accelerating.

"Aren't you bored all the time? There's absolutely nothing to do here."

"There's plenty to do."

"Are you serious?"

"Yeah."

She stared at him as if awaiting further explanation. When he failed to speak, she said, "California must have been exciting. You miss it like crazy, right?"

"Not really. Duluth is just like Sacramento. Trees, water, rocks."

"You have trees, water, and rocks in your head."

"Nothing wrong with that," he said, turning without signaling.

"And snow on your brain."

"I love snow. I can't wait."

"Oh, give me a break." Pixie gave him a little pout. "Don't you wanna fly away to some exotic place?"

"Here we are," Chris said, slamming on the brakes in front of Sunshine Laundromat. "Duluth is exotic in its own way. Duluth has everything that I love."

"Okay, fine, good for you. But do you know what I love?"

The words made him catch his breath. Was she going to declare her love for him? That might complicate things, and yet hearing such a declaration was something he desired.

"I love birds," Pixie said. "I love them more than anything."

"Um, ah, that's great. Because here we are, on a Friday night, at a laundromat with birds."

The teenagers went into Sunshine, one eagerly and one half-heartedly. The cheerleader ran toward the aviary and began chirping at Chipper, a blue parakeet. He chirped back though the cage, "Pretty girl, pretty girl."

"Oh, so sweet. Pretty bird, pretty bird."

"Pretty girl," Chipper repeated happily, "pretty girl,

pretty girl."

Spit!

Duane Schmidt, cradling his sloppy Coke can, was seated in a chair near the dryers. He slurred at Chris, "Word on the street says you scored, Lake."

"Oh, hey there, Dip."

The spitter gestured toward the cheerleader. "Scored during and after the game, eh?"

Several birds made a fluttering commotion while Chris scampered forward and lowered his shoulder. The muscles in his legs sprung with such anger that the chair and Dip went crashing all the way over to a washing machine. The can full of spit splattered on Dip's face and shirt, and a trickle of blood ran out of his mouth.

The sight of the blood made Chris's wrath turn to contrition. "Ah, man. Sorry, Duane."

"Yes, we are sorry," Pixie said, holding a tissue. She dabbed at the drooler's mouth and scolded him. "But you shouldn't have baited Chris. Why did you do that? Why are you here?"

Dip smiled, revealing a bloody gap between his teeth. "Your boyfriend's all done playing football. He's finished. And so are you."

Chapter Forty-Four

Monday, bloody Monday, Chris was called into Coach Lundblat's office. "Turn in your uniform, Lake. You're off the team—for fighting."

"You want to hear my side of the story? And Pixie's side of the story?"

Lundblat chomped his gum and pounded his desk. "I invested a whole season in you! Just a sophomore. I let you have the ball while juniors and seniors sat on the bench. Do you know how many angry phone calls I got, complaining about you and your showboating?"

"Showboating?"

"Kicking up your legs like a half-assed dancer. I allowed it because you were scoring." Chomp, chomp. "But I never liked it."

Chris recalled some of his highlights, those moments of temporary glory. "People complained about me? I just ran—as best I could. You could've coached me more."

"You're saying it's my fault? "Lundblat raged around the desk. "If you want to challenge me, just punch me in the face."

"Huh?"

He stuck out his chomping chin. "Punch me, showboat."

So tempting. "And if I do, am I back on the team?"

Lundblat tried to think, not expecting such a question. "Um, no," he said. "But I'll give you ten dollars."

"What?"

Chomp, chomp. "I'll give you ten dollars if you punch me."

The worst thing one can do is laugh at a coach. And that's exactly what Chris did, guffawing uncontrollably. And he also spoke a dangerous truth. "I heard Dip's father threatened your job."

Lundblat raised his fist. "That's a lie."

"Then what's the truth? Why are you kicking me off the team?"

Chomp, chomp. "For fighting."

"Fighting?"

"Yeah."

"But coach," Chris said, trying to keep a straight face,

"you're trying to fight me now."

"What? Exactly. That's why you're off the team."

"Because you started a fight with me?"

"Yeah. I mean—get out of here, Lake! You don't want to listen to reason. You only believe what you want to believe." Chomp, chomp. "Go on, get. I have playoffs to prepare for." Chomp, chomp. Swallow. "For crap sake."

Chapter Forty-Five

November dropping a dangerous snowstorm, Chris found Pixie in Majestic, gave her a little kiss, and said, "Where to?"

"Anywhere."

The girl's face was ashen, eyes red and half-hidden beneath a rumpled gray hoodie. "Drive me downtown. Or up the shore. It doesn't matter."

"Okay. Fasten your seat belt."

"No."

"The roads are bad. We need to be careful."

"I don't feel like it."

"Fine." Chris leaned across her body and fastened the belt for her. "There you are. We're good to go."

"Go," she said. "Get me out of here."

"Okay."

The boy lightly revved the engine and Majestic sputtered away, fighting the wind, wobbling, almost veering into the wrong lane a few times. Keeping both hands on the wheel, Chris drove toward downtown, turning onto Superior Street.

"Slow down!" Pixie said. "Look—there's a deer on your right."

"I see it."

"And another deer—right there."

Chris stopped the car, admiring the animals. "A buck and a doe. Glorious—in their own way. Right?"

Pixie rolled down the window and shouted, "Go back to the woods! Get out of here! Go home!"

The two deer stood happily on the sidewalk. They had little desire to return to the woods, at least not during hunting season. They liked the city. There was lots of food and life was good when they weren't getting hit by cars.

"They'll be okay," Chris said, knowing he couldn't promise such a thing. All he could do was not hit the deer himself. "They'll be okay," he repeated, wishing he actually believed that.

"They're gonna get killed," Pixie said. "They're gonna get slaughtered. Some drunk driver will—"

"C'mon, try to think good thoughts." Chris flicked

on the headlights and eased away from the snow-kissed animals, wondering where he could bring Pixie that would make her happy. Maybe Sunshine?

"Don't bring me to Sunshine," the girl said. "That place makes me sad."

"Um, okay. Where you wanna go?"

"Just drive. Please stop talking, Christopher. Just drive the damn car. Anywhere. Except Sunshine. I hate that place."

"Okay."

Meandering around downtown Duluth for a while, watching pedestrians lean into the strengthening gale of a growing blizzard, Chris waited for Pixie to say something, anything, the silence feeling like a sort of death in the car. He sighed loudly at every stoplight, not knowing what to say; and when the light turned eerie green, he didn't know where to go, so eventually Christopher just let Majestic cross over to Canal Park. The boy glanced at Pixie's face and was increasingly worried by the paleness and trembling lips—it seemed like she was muttering curses.

"You okay, Pix?"

"Stop the car and park here," she said. "Let's go for a walk—onto the lift-bridge."

"You sure? In this weather?"

"I'm sure." And away she went, stumbling and slipping into the tempest.

Chris felt a chill that had nothing to do with the weather. It was a feeling worse than the deathly silence of the drive.

"Pix! Pixie, wait up!"

Wind whipped down from the north, causing wild waves to crash into the canal. Mist was turning to ice, slicking the steel bridge. "Hey, wait. Pix! Let's go to the bakery and get something warm."

She turned too quickly, flailing, almost falling. Her eyes were livid. "You think all I need is a pastry? Give the girl flour and sugar, and everything will be fine? What's wrong with you? Can't you see my life's gone down the toilet? First, I get kicked off the cheerleading squad because you fought with Duane. Now the other cheerleaders won't even speak to me, like it's my fault we lost the play-off game. And then my mom moves to Missouri and leaves me with my drunk father who's having an affair with a waitress who just turned twenty-three. I heard him on the phone today saying something about an abortion. And you think a pastry is the answer?"

Chris wrapped his arms around her. "I'm sorry. I didn't know things were that bad."

She squirmed away and turned to face the face-blasting gale. "It doesn't matter. Don't be sorry. We tried our best."

We tried our best? The boy was confused. Those words suggested they'd just broken up. Had they even been together? *For real?*

The two kids stood shivering, the freezing mist coating their hair like years of aging, until the warning bells on the bridge began to ring, announcing that a ship was coming in and the bridge would soon be rising into the raging sky.

"What are you doing for Christmas?" Chris asked, taking her hand and leading her back to Majestic. "Any plans?"

"No plans," Pixie said, her face all ghostly. "No expectations. No disappointments."

Chapter Forty-Six

On Christmas Eve, with *Angels We Have Heard on High* stuck in an amplified loop, Chris and Pixie stood in the downtown Skywalk, suspended above Superior Street. The frosty glass windows made the Skywalk seem like a hollow icicle.

"This is cool," the boy said, knowing it wasn't.

"I hate it," Pixie replied. She was dressed in a red coat and green pants, a surface of festivity. "Everything sucks."

"Oh. Well, um, wanna go to church?"

Her eyes filled with tears and anger. "My parents always went to church on Christmas. And look where it got them."

Chris gave her a hug and wanted to give her all the hope in the world—or as much hope as he currently had. "We could go to my house. It might be okay. My parents will drive us crazy, but not insane."

Pixie wiped a tear, almost laughing. "I guess crazy's good enough tonight."

God, please don't let it be insane. Please, don't let it be insane. God, please...

"Happy Solstice!"

Val, wearing every color of the hippie rainbow, stood in the open door and waved the kids inside. "I have steaming chai, ginseng, and synthetic octopus to warm you up!"

"Oh, my." Pixie felt like crying and laughing and ended up giving Val a gracious smile. "Merry Christmas, Mrs. Lake."

"Come in, come in! We have the fireplace stoked."

Chris whispered in the girl's ear, "They might actually be stoked."

"Yikes," she replied, giggling, venturing deeper into the strange cheer. It was wonderfully cozy by the fireplace; and it was great fun to sample both the chai and ginseng; and the candied synthetic octopus pieces were actually edible; and the sitar music created an otherworldly ambience that almost seemed appropriate for the occasion.

"This is amazingly nice," Pixie said. "Thank you for letting me be here."

Joe wore tie-die and a mischievous grin. "Young lady, I've heard you have an interest in birds. Especially tropical ones."

"Um, yeah," Pixie said, beaming. "That's true."

"So. You'll be able to take care of them?"

"What do you mean, take care of them?"

Val slipped out of the room, obviously on a mission.

"What's going on?" Pixie asked. "I feel like I'm dreaming."

"We have a present for you," Joe said. "Topher was talking about you the other day and the idea just seemed obvious."

The girl grabbed the boy's arm. "What are you doing? I didn't expect anything."

He shrugged. "Low expectations. High dividends."

"Blessings, blessings!" Val returned to the living room with a golden cage full of chirping.

"Birds!" the girl cheered.

"Birds, indeed." Val placed the golden present on Pixie's lap. The girl immediately began cooing at the plum-headed parakeets. "Ohh, so beautiful. Ohh, I love you, I love you."

"Merry Christmas," Chris said, and added with a whisper, "Well done, Mom and Dad."

Hugging the cage, Pixie tried not to cry, but there was no stopping the joyful tears. "This is the best gift," she said. "Thank you, thank you. I can't believe you did this for me."

Val and Joe gave each other satisfied looks, the sitar music played itself out, and the night became silent—except for the birdsong. There were other presents under the Solstice tree, but nobody felt the need to distribute them.

"What's better than birds?" Pixie said.

Chapter Forty-Seven

In the morning, Chris received a Gibson guitar, strings shimmering. He high-fived his parents, glanced at the instruction book, then spent Christmas Day in his room, strumming and humming melodies. Sometimes he stared out the window at a heart-shaped mountain of snow, searching for a song in there. *Buried, buried, still breathing...* He wanted to give voice to that buried song, but first he had to master notes and chords and progressions. Notes and chords and progressions.

His cell phone rang. He paused, then picked up. "Hey, Pix."

"Chris, the birds are amazing! I just sit around watching them. I love how they drink water. It's so cute. And Rio is such a flirt. She chirps whenever Belize is looking away. Check this out, when my dad left the house today, I let the birds out of the cage to stretch their wings. After a few swoops through the living room, Rio roosted on the kitchen table and Belize claimed the top of the fridge. And they sang to each other."

The guitar graced the boy's knees and he strummed random strings while listening to her rhapsody.

"I walked to Sunshine this morning to thank the manager for letting your parents buy the birds, but the guy wasn't there. Can you guess who was cleaning the aviary?"

"Was it Dip?"

"Don't be silly."

"Moosehead? Skunk?"

"Guess again."

Chris strummed, trying to find better intuition. "Was it an angel?"

"Don't be sacrilegious."

"I imagine angels clean up lots of things. Why not an aviary?"

"Dude, control your imagination."

"If I control my imagination, I can't guess who you saw in Sunshine."

The girl sighed, giving up the game. "It was Trevor."

Strum, strum. "Who's Trevor?"

"You know, sort of thin and serious, always talking about God. Kind of cute."

"Oh, yeah, Trevor. I like him. I broke his glasses and he forgave me. Now he wears contacts and the chicks dig him. Including my chick, apparently."

"Your chick? Haha. Listen. Are you listening?"

Strum, strum. "I'm all ears."

"Chris, I want to ask you out."

"Cool."

"There's a party at Sacred Heart Community Center on New Year's Eve."

"How'd you hear about it? Did the cute God-boy invite you?"

"Well, um..."

"So. This is a date with you and me and Trevor Nelson?"

"No. This is just three people going to Sacred Heart."

"Whatever."

"It'll be awesome. They've been doing cool things at the community center. Trevor says—"

"God be with you."

"No, he doesn't. I mean—"

"Bye."

"Okay. Bye."

Click.

Notes and chords and progressions. Notes and chords and progressions...

Chapter Forty-Eight

Val and Joe had mountains of vinyl records, and Chris explored them all, visualizing the seemingly magical fingers that could create such sounds. How did the guitarists play with such extraordinary power?

"Turn that crap down!" Joe shouted from his office. He pounded the wall, protesting his own music. "I'm trying to get work done!"

"Sorry."

Chris put on the headphones and considered Led Zeppelin, Jefferson Airplane, Jimi Hendrix, The Grateful Dead...and settled on Bach.

His parents had only one classical album in their collection: *Four Lute Suites*.

"Is it four lutes? Or four suites? Or both? Hmm." He

lowered the needle and noticed nothing extraordinary in the playing. In fact, at first, Chris was a bit bored with the progressions. The lute player seemed talented enough, but where was the passion? Where was the love? The boy was about to remove Bach from the turntable and put on The Who when a series of hushed, simple notes gave him pause. And his heart began to pound.

"Okay, fine," he muttered as if he'd lost an argument. "I'll go to Sacred Heart."

Chapter Forty-Nine

New Year's Eve, Chris picked up Pixie and drove her to the community center. It was a former church located halfway between her house and the harbor, a Gothic Revival barely saved from demolition, a brownstone beauty with a great spire, now the center of the local arts scene. Festoons of lights at the entrance suggested a welcoming realm for all, and Pixie sprang forward from the car the moment it stopped. "Trevor!" She rushed up the steps to a grinning geek, his head haloed by disco lights.

"Hey, girl," Trevor said. "Welcome to paradise."

She gave him a hug. "Tonight's the big night."

"Yes. Everything's arranged."

"Arranged?" Chris trailed the lovebirds into the ambiguously sacred space, wondering why he'd accepted this invitation. *I'm the non-date on their date...because I thought the lutes told me to do this...Bach, O Bach, you done me wrong.* Inside the center, he slouched in the back and pensively watched as Pixie and Trevor joined the dance. They danced as if outside of time, timeless in some perfect timing. He actually tried to be happy for them, sort of, and wondered about their exchange of smiles that signified something beyond flesh.

"Whooo-hooo!" they said.

The light show intensified an hour before midnight with laser beams seemingly shattering the stained glass and yet leaving it unbroken. All was a colorful, whirling, cosmic blur, and the ex-cheerleader couldn't help herself. She laughed and shouted and praised the Lord—with freaking Trevor Nelson.

"Looks like she finally has a soulmate," Chris muttered, and went outside for a smoke. He'd brought a whole pack of Swisher Sweets, thinking other uncomfortable guys would join him in the parking lot. He lit up alone, staring into the star fields, his breath making melancholy clouds. Christopher smoked one cigar after another, shivering, but not coughing, snuffing out his fourth just before midnight. He returned to the party a bit woozy, seeing all the boys and girls pairing up in the wild lights and licking their lips for the ritual kiss. The ex-football star stood by himself in the back of the ex-church, squinting and searching, squinting and searching...for what?

"Ten, nine, eight!" Pixie shouted, leaping up and down.

Chris thought about rushing onto the dance floor and claiming her for the kiss. That would show Trevor who was boss.

"...five, four, three..."

He recalled the touchdowns, the cheers, the accolades.

"HAPPY NEW YEAR!"

You've got to be kidding me.

Trevor, smooching Pixie like a geek in need of eternal celibacy, had utterly defeated him.

Chapter Fifty

When Val Lake smelled tobacco on her son's clothing and saw a pack of cigars on his dresser, she wept all night.

Joe eventually woke up and noticed the weeping. "What's wrong?"

"Topher's wrong. He's bent on destroying his thyroid. With Swisher Sweets! I can't bear it. He's losing his body-spirit balance, lurching toward the abyss! Why are you laughing?"

"Because, um, we've done our share of smoking. And we, um, turned out fine."

"But Topher's different. He doesn't need to make our mistakes. He has something inside that's especially special. Our Topher is the Chosen One. Isn't he?"

Joe laughed heartily and gave his wife a big hug. "Topher's going through a phase. He'll become a good, healthy man. Don't worry."

She sniffled. "Will he give me healthy grandchildren?"

"Not sure I can promise that, babe."

"Well, I've been feeding him a ton of cabbage. It boosts testosterone."

"Yikes."

Chapter Fifty-One

Chris spent the rest of his sophomore year fantasizing during class, smoking in the woods afterwards, and practicing guitar chords all night—ascending and descending...

In order to pass his English class, he had to write an extra-credit paper.

A FANTASY THAT COULD BE TRUE

There are angels in Lake Superior. Like great leviathans, they lurk and frolic a thousand feet down. Larger than wooly mammoths, more powerful than icebergs, the angels of Superior absorb invisible rays of sunlight, moonlight, starlight, and especially the Northern Lights.

Full of light in the depths, the angels guard the sunken ships and treasures. And they sing and leap out of the lake when nobody's looking. You should see the colorful droplets fall from their crowns above the harbor, upon all the houses on the hill. The angels swim toward the moon that turns blue at the sight of such things. And ship captains on the verge of becoming ghosts get all trembly, because it's time to sink, swim, or sing—with the angels.

The end.

Mr. Kendall wrote on the paper. "Not a bad vision. Strong imagery and good sense of motion. The story swims nicely. You certainly have a unique style. I just wish you'd written the full three pages of the assignment. D+"

Chapter Fifty-Two

Sweet, sad summer found Chris almost six-feet tall and sporting whiskers that aged him a few years. He wore dark sunglasses, day and night, and felt like he was old enough to visit bars for live music. The first time he tried that, in a downtown dive called Downtown Dive, he just sauntered in and sat in a chair in the back corner. The on-stage performer was a grizzled guy chugging Budweiser while gravel-voicing through covers of Glen Campbell, James Taylor, Carly Simon, Joan Baez, and The Monkees. After a jaded, off-key rendition of *I'm a Believer*, the guy staggered into the dank bathroom.

Of the seven people in the bar, Chris was the only one to applaud. "Bravo! Bravo!"

The toilet flushed, and flushed again.

"Bravo!" Chris strode over to the bartender. "Excuse me, sir—"

The burly old man flung a dirty towel over his shoulder. "Sir? Nope. My name's Hurley. Now show me your ID, mister shades."

Lies of various believability buzzed in the teen's mind. He was fairly confident he could fool Hurley. However, he confessed, "I'm not quite seventeen. Sir."

The bartender sighed and pointed his dirty towel at the door. "Get out."

"All I want is a pen, sir. No whiskey, no bourbon, no vodka, no tequila, not even a beer. I just want to write a few verses. This place is inspiring."

Burley Hurley shook his head, started to point at the door again, and chuckled. "Never had a writer in here—unless you count them limericks on the bathroom walls. Can't understood why anyone would wanna write anything. But, um, knock yourself out." He handed over a rusty, bar-stained pen.

"Thanks, Hurley—sir."

"Yeah, you sit in the corner and write. But if you cause any trouble, kid, I'll rip out your guts and fry 'em in the fryer."

"It's a deal."

Chris returned to his seat while the performer returned from the toilet. Another song ensued, *Harvest Moon* by Neil

Young, and Chris free-associated his own lyrics, scribbling on beer napkins. He wrote about aurora mysteries, hummingbirds, and mountain lions, a mix of worldly and heavenly images. The crappy old pen soon ran out of ink, and he tossed the napkins into the garbage.

"Bravo!" he called over his shoulder while leaving, thinking it was one of the best nights of his life.

The rest of the summer, Chris became a pub crawler, charming his way across the music scene, from Lakeview Castle to the Buffalo House. He'd reached the point that he could simply say to his parents, "I'm going out," and they didn't ask any questions, as long as he returned by midnight, not smelling of smoke.

Majestic managed to keep running—sputtering—from haunt to haunt where Chris sought out the hidden, unsung, singer-songwriters who'd dedicated their lives to musing on the dangers and delights of existence. Most evenings, the performers were average and forgettable, yet Chris always applauded. And he had a strange, incessant belief that he'd be summoned to the stage—at any given moment—so he always kept his Gibson in the car.

One night at Lakeview Castle, Chris was scribbling nonsense on a napkin, yawning, not paying attention to the music, when he was struck by a beam of light from the stage. He took off his sunglasses and stared directly into the light, thinking: *This is it. This is it. But what...is it?*

It was inspiration. It was not coming from the stage. And it was gone.

Chapter Fifty-Three

The next night, at Amazing Grace Café, a woman with an electric cello seemed to have a whole universe of inspiration in her strings—or at least all of Lake Superior. Schools of silvery fish filled her music, swim-flying above the surface, while trilling gulls ghosted through the mist.

Chris wept when the music was over. He felt like he'd been drowned in a great cloud of artistic mastery.

He wiped his tears, cleaned his sunglasses, and stumbled out to the car. He fired up Majestic and sped up the dark hillside. He parked beside the Ruins, reached into the back seat for his guitar—and kissed it goodbye. Knowing he'd never be able to lyricize those strings properly, Chris placed the Gibson on a broken stone beneath the archway. He paused for a moment, a sort of prayer of sacrifice, and hoped the unmerited gift would be carried off by first light.

It was.

Chapter Fifty-Four

"Do you miss it?" Pixie asked, strolling under autumn trees with Chris after school.

She knows? About the music?

"Miss what?" he asked.

"You know, the blood and the glory."

Oh, football.

"I never bled," Chris said, "and scoring a touchdown isn't much glory."

The girl smiled. "I don't miss football, either. Hey, can you keep walking with me?"

"Of course," Chris said, touching her hand, wanting to hold it, and letting it go. "Where we going?"

"It's a surprise. C'mon."

Through the corridor of gold and scarlet leaves, and

winding down several blocks through pines and firs ever pining for Christmas, Pixie led him to Superior Street and down the sidewalk for another few blocks to a bookstore housed in a former brewery, an old beauty of brick and mortar. There she purchased a golden pen and a packet of fancy stationery.

"What's that for?" he asked.

She handed him the goods. "Happy birthday!"

"You remembered."

"Of course I remembered. Seventeen!"

"These are excellent presents," he said, trying to sound happy but feeling distraught at the thought of writing. "Thank you."

"I think you'll be a great writer," Pixie said, grinning. "You have a deep heart."

"Everyone has a deep heart."

"Well, yeah. But you're special."

"Okay, Mom."

The two friends left the store laughing, moving slowly, enjoying each other's company, and then paused on the leafy sidewalk. The air smelled of decay and fresh air blowing in from the lake, a mix of death and life and something else. The birthday boy, feeling inspired, kissed Pixie on the cheek. She seemed to like it, so he tried for the lips.

She pulled away. "You should join the Bible study.

There's still time."

"Bible study?" Chris put on his sunglasses. "Trevor's Bible study? Ah, no thank you." He craned his neck toward the lake. "Do you hear that? I believe I'm being called to study scripture."

"Don't be a jerk," Pixie said, pouting. "I guess I'll talk to you tomorrow."

"For sure. Thanks again for the presents. And give my regards to Saint Trevor."

"Whatever. Go study the lake. And write." She smiled half-angrily and waved him away. "Oh, wait a sec."

"What?"

"The stationery is for writing letters. Special letters. And it is good for poems, too. Because the best poems are letters, right? Letters from the soul to the world."

"I guess so. If you say so."

"I say so. Bye."

"Bye, Pix."

Gifts in hand, but without inspiration, Chris shuffled through the leaves to the lake, thinking he could at least contemplate poetic possibilities. Reclining on a grassy slope, he thought he might scribble something about shimmering stones in shallow water, how they patiently await storms to carry them to shore or out to the deeps. Christopher began to touch pen to paper when wild wailing demanded his attention. At first he thought the wailing was coming from within, something metaphysical, or a manifestation of emotional turmoil, but he soon realized it was just a loon on the lake. Or rather two loons. Invisible. *Where are they? Where are they?* The birds wailed again—somewhere between water and sky—their ancient song of songs of the north, and Chris tried to spell out the sounds on a piece of stationery, combining vowels in various ways to render his version of a psalm or poetic epistle. He scribbled furiously for a while, enthralled by the flow of words, and then more slowly, and suddenly stopping, the ecstasy of inspiration scourged by the pen losing it on paper. "Augh." Chris could not capture the meaning of the laughing, mourning, invisible, winged creatures.

Father Hopkins. Did you suffer like this? Or was it easy for you?

The birthday boy crumpled the fine stationery into a ball and cast it upon the water. "All yours, Superior." His creative failure bobbed in the shallows for a while, and began drifting toward the deep waters, slowly expanding in the light like a chunk of bread.

Chapter Fifty-Five

Chris abstained from writing and learned how to fix cars, taking Majestic apart and putting the whole thing back together; and he did the same for his parents, impressing them with his mechanical abilities and giving Joe hope that his son would never be homeless.

"Topher, buddy," he said, nodding happily in the garage, "I really hate getting my hands dirty—as do millions of other people. So if you want to be a grease monkey, I'm all for it, as long as you own the business. Don't be someone else's monkey."

"Um, okay, Dad."

Machines filled Christopher's days and dreams, and he stopped thinking about songs and poems and the depths of his soul—until another New Year's Eve when he felt the call again. Alone at a coffee shop open mic, he felt inspired, and tortured, while watching an Emo Girl emoting in a black dress and fish-net stockings. Chris sat near the stage, staring at the remaining pages of the stationary Pix had given him. *Apocalypse not now,* he wrote in large letters, *Apocalypse later, please.*

"See your shadow at midnight," Emo Girl intoned, and disappeared.

Next at the mic was a clean-cut boy in a sweatshirt. "Hey. I'm Kyle." He sat on a stool and crooned about deer hunting with his grandpa. After the sentimental deer was shot and made into jerky—a process that took two verses—the song trailed off into the final chorus: "*Gramps loved venison jerky almost as much as Grams. And love like that always gives a damn, always gives a damn—dang it—love like that made Gramps the man.*" Kyle smiled at the audience, some of whom applauded, relating to the message, and he said, "I have some CDs for sale. Actually, boxes and boxes of CDs. So, if you want to buy one, or something. Yeah. Maybe for Christmas next year. Or if anyone ever has a birthday, give me a holler."

Chris wrote in larger letters, filling a page: *How do you lead a deer to still waters? Let it leap, let it leap, let it leap...*

A long-haired geezer meandered up to the microphone. He had a battered guitar with a harmonica duct-taped to a rusty frame and he performed a song about hopping freight trains. "*I'm just a piece of iron ore,*" the geezer sang, "*an unrefined hobo, rollin' up the North Shore!*"

"Bravo! Bravo!" Chris was a big fan of that song and drew a picture of a new superhero: *The Unrefined Hobo (with a Heart of Gold)*. He thought maybe he could make a comic book—but he was running out of stationary.

A sweet lullaby-girl entered the spotlight and swayed as if in a mystical breeze, her lilting voice searching for an everlasting harmony. "*I'm searching, searching,*" she sang, "*for an everlasting harmony, an everlasting song, and a prom, and a party—and you're searching for me. You should've gone to the prom with meee.*"

Chris filled another page:

She swoons for amore
and more
unable
to find
the unfathomable
dying
to meet her
at Love's everlasting table

"No, that's not it," he muttered, crumpling it up. He sipped more coffee and tried again:

Her search is an invitation

to her own heart
to sing the original song
already singing
in harmony
for the soul everlasting

"Ugh." He crumpled the page and tossed it in disgust, almost hitting a new performer approaching the stage. Chris was about to call it a night, another disappointing year, when he looked toward the microphone and saw a familiar face, and heard a familiar voice, accompanied by the guitar he'd abandoned at the Ruins.

Mary Joan Mudgett, in a white dress, was playing her first gig, strumming and singing, "*The lion of the northland sleeps in a roaring dream, doorway to fields within forests of green and blue. Don't go there, boy. Don't go there, boy. Unless you bring your roar of dreaming, unless you bring your roar of dreaming.*"

At the end of the song, Mary Joan received the most applause of the night and a harmony of respect from Kyle and the geezer who hollered like refined hobos, "Encore! Encore!" The girl bowed graciously. "Thank you. That's all I have." She descended the stage and tried to whisk away from her admirers, but Chris was able to stop her with his compliment. "You play my guitar better than I ever did."

"Christopher! Hi! What do you mean, your guitar?"

He laughed and pointed, "Yep. That's my Gibson."

"No, it isn't."

"My name's on it."

Mary Joan half-smiled and peered at him, wondering what sort of game he was playing. "I don't believe you."

"Wanna bet? I'll bet you anything."

She held out her hand. "Okay, it's a bet. Anything."

They shook, and Chris grabbed the guitar and held it to the light. He examined it intently, but his name was not there.

"Pay up," the girl said. "I want a Stratocaster."

"Wait. Just wait a sec." Chris angled the guitar, this way and that, trying to catch the light just right.

"There! Look!"

Mary Joan didn't want to look, but she forced herself to glance. And there, under the shine, very faint, was a slight scratch. The boy's name.

Chapter Fifty-Six

The cellist with water-music in her strings began playing toward midnight, stirring many in the audience to dance to that wonderful resonance. Christopher swayed not far from Mary Joan, and whispered, "I was joking about the bet. You keep the guitar."

She danced closer, almost touching him. "You won fair and square. That guitar was yours all along."

"I don't care about the guitar," he said, putting his arms around her. The couple moved more slowly to the music. "I've missed you, Mary Joan."

The girl didn't reply, but he assumed the feeling was mutual, whatever that feeling was. *Not love*, he thought, *and yet...maybe...more than friendship?*

When the water-music ended on a note that seemed to

flow on, Mary Joan gave him the sweetest smile, not flirty, just perfectly sweet. "The whole family has missed you, Christopher."

Hmm...more than friendship? Famship?

"Grant and Chastity still talk about how bad you were at milking goats and playing the Word Game. Mother says you're gonna star on Broadway—musicals." The girl paused, laughing. "And my dad, who hates all potential boyfriends, has never spoken ill of you. That's sort of a miracle."

"Oh. Cool." Chris grinned nervously and tried to figure out what to do about the impending New Year's ritual. He'd made such a mess of things on the cruise, and now he had ten seconds to make a decision. *Kiss her hand like a gentleman? I don't want to lead her on. Yet...what if she wants a real kiss? Should I—"*

Three, two, one!

"HAPPY NEW YEAR!"

Emo Girl planted lips on Kyle.

Lullaby Girl got smooched by a random romantic.

"Woo-woo!" The long-haired geezer kissed his harmonica.

Mary Joan, so gorgeous in her white dress, like an image of some saintly goddess, took a step away from her non-date and extended her hand—not to be kissed—and the boy shook it, sealing the deal.

Just friends.

"Have a great year," she said.

"Um, okay," Chris muttered, letting go, "same to you."

Chapter Fifty-Seven

Senior year, Chris decided to forget girls and focus on money.

He devised a business plan, revised it, and showed it to his father.

Joe's home office was a chaos of blinking computers and financial news blaring from a large-screen TV.

"I don't like these numbers, Topher. You've overpriced the product and underpriced the cost of production."

"So, it's not a good plan?"

Joe frowned. "Mugs? You wanna sell mugs? What the hell inspired that idea? Have you started drinking vodka? Smoking dope?"

Chris laughed. "Nope."

"Help me out here, son. I can't catch the vision if you

can't paint me a picture."

"Paint you a picture?" Staring at his father's cluttered desk, the aspiring millionaire tried to remember how he'd gotten the idea for the mugs. He mumbled, "I saw a kid slobbering."

"Your plan began with slobbering?"

"There's a kid at school, Dip—"

"The kid you fought. At the laundromat."

"We didn't fight. I tackled him. Anyway, he's always drooling into a can. It's sort of gross."

"Sort of? It's really, really, really gross. What that kid needs is a spittoon."

"A spittoon? What the heck is a spittoon?"

Joe laughed, loving an opportunity to give a little lecture. "In the old days, before the 60s cleaned things up, millions of people were spitting—all over. They had spittoons everywhere, shaped like trophy cups. They were usually made of brass, decorating hotel lobbies, train cars, restaurants. Seriously, in the old days, people were spitting everywhere."

"You think a spittoon would solve Dip's problem?"

"You tell me, son. You're the visionary."

"Well, a spittoon isn't what I'm envisioning. I mean, yeah, Dip needs something like that. But my mugs aren't targeted at spitters. My mugs are for entertainment. And social satire."

"Satire," Joe said, "like *Saturday Night Live*? Back when it was funny? Before it got so bad they should all be arrested?"

"Exactly. Mug Shot Mugs."

"Huh?"

"Look at the last page of my business plan. Look at the sample images."

Flipping through the pages, Joe muttered, "Hmm. Hmm. Well, maybe. Okay, I think I get it. Hey, that's pretty funny. It's a police mug shot. On a coffee mug."

"Yep."

"Hmm. I like it, Topher."

"Thanks. Now look at the smaller image—on the next page."

"A mug shot on a shot glass. Huh. That's clever."

"You think?"

"I think," Joe said, shaking his son's hand. "I think we have a deal."

Chris grinned. "Okay, we have a deal."

"Seventy—thirty," Joe said.

"Oh, you deserve more than thirty percent, Dad. You're putting up all of the capital."

The old hippie nodded. "I'm getting the seventy."

"Oh. Right."

Chapter Fifty-Eight

The mugs and shot glasses featured the faces of arrested celebrities. Along with Nick Nolte, other bestsellers included Jane Fonda, Hugh Grant, Paris Hilton, James Brown, and Pee-wee Herman. All sales were online, the shipments sent out from a warehouse in Minneapolis. The Lake boys didn't have to do much except watch their sales double and triple and quadruple. With thirty percent of the net earnings, Chris was swimming in cash.

"You should buy a house," his mother said, handing him a shot of chai.

The young entrepreneur took Jane Fonda into his hands. "Trying to get rid of me?"

"Get rid of you?" She sipped from a James Brown mug. "Not yet."

"What would I do with a house?"

"We'd decorate it. And increase its value."

"Yeah? You and me, Mom?"

Val smoothed a wrinkle on her lime sari. "You're growing up so fast, Topher. I'd like a chance to work on a project with you, before you journey into the cosmos to achieve more fame and fortune. Your father says you're some kind of genius."

Chris laughed. "Seriously?"

"Seriously." Val sipped her tea and gave him a smile. "I'm thinking about seeing fewer patients. I want to spend more time with you. We'll revitalize an old house, like that stone cottage on Third Street. I'll do the fun stuff like painting walls, putting up crown molding, and hanging drapes. You can do the dirty work like putting in new toilets and finding renters."

"Gee, thanks, Mom."

"Anytime, my genius boy."

Val helped him buy the stone cottage, closing the deal and signing the final documents by the middle of October. The next thirty days were some of the happiest of Christopher's life, working on renovations with his funny, creative mother. They agreed to keep the style historical because, Val said, "The same colors I saw at Woodstock were also enjoyed in Bohemia in the 1360s." Mother and child laughed and colored each other's faces with little dabs while painting the formal dining room red and orange. "It's not war paint," Christopher declared. "You're right," Val said, "it's peace paint." And without washing it off, they went shopping and found yellow-gold chairs at Goodwill, apparently discarded by a medieval-renaissance festival. "Worthy of banquets," the boy said. "Oh, yes," his mom agreed, "for lords and ladies—and me."

Later in the renovation process, after new toilets were installed, they hung a chandelier that sparkled like a spiraling galaxy. "Oh my stars," Val said, weeping with joy. "Topher, please don't ever sell this place. Keep this house forever and forevermore."

Chapter Fifty-Nine

"Sell that thing," his father said.

The real-estate market was upswinging, and Joe calculated that Chris could make a profit of twenty-thousand dollars. "And with good decisions, you'll have a million dollars by the time you're thirty. And two million when you're fifty. And retire like a king."

Thinking his father knew best, Chris planted a "For Sale by Owner" sign in front of the stone cottage. "I'm not happy about this," he whispered, and he dreaded the conversation later with his mom. "I don't know if they do thyroid replacements, but I think she'll need a new one. Frick. Why is everything so complicated?" After whispering his complaints to the leafless, Autumn trees, he walked slowly up the hill, careful to keep on the edge of the narrow road. Occasionally he kicked pebbles over a cliff and listened to them clack on the boulders below—except one pebble traveled further than expected, ricocheting upon a house with a sound that suggested breakage, maybe a solar panel or terra cotta tile.

Chris peered over the ledge. Hundreds of homes graced the hillside, and it would be impossible to figure out which roof had taken the hit.

Shit!

Being a homeowner himself, he thought he should go down and knock on the door of every house, asking if anyone had suffered damage.

Forever. That would take forever.

Sighing, Chris sat on the cliffside, feet dangling, waiting to see if anybody came out of a house cursing and shaking a fist at the sky. After several hours, witnessing no raging, he took that as a sign that no harm had been done. And yet he felt guilty.

Please, help me to be more careful. I never want to be the one causing damage.

Chapter Sixty

The first snowfall was a whirling glory, filling Duluth like a painting of light—light upon light—but Chris was depressed on Thanksgiving. He slouched in his home, staring at a computer screen. His father had convinced him to sell the mug company. Ka-ching! Ka-ching! Thirty percent of the transaction resulted in a hundred-thousand dollars.

Sigh.

Click.

The computer screen faded into darkness. The rich young man closed his eyes and wondered how rich he'd be when the cottage finally sold. He felt an old ache in his chest, and heard his mother call happily up the stairs, "Sweetie, time to eat! Wash up!"

"Frick."

Not bothering to wash, Chris plodded down the stairs and took his place at the table. It was all decked out in bountiful colors for the colorless meal. Val had made the traditional Thanksgiving feast: turkey tofu.

"Beautiful!" Joe exclaimed. He was in high spirits because of the sale of the company.

Chris growled, "Why can't we have real meat today? And mashed potatoes and gravy? And cornbread and strawberry jam?"

"Don't be a downer," his mother chided with extra joy. "Don't you know what the Dalai Lama said?"

"The Chinese are killing me."

"That's not funny."

Joe laughed. "Well, the Chinese might kill our economy. You think they bought any of our mugs? Hell no. Apparently they find no humor in Pee-wee Herman."

"The Dalai Lama has reminded our souls," Val said, bowing over a tofu leg, "to always be grateful."

"Yeah," Chris muttered, "I'd be grateful for some real meat. I'd even settle for green-bean casserole with bacon bits."

"Thank you, universe! Oh, thanks be to you!" Val lifted a morsel to her mouth. "No more talking nonsense about bacon bits. Eat up!"

"Oh, crap." Joe's phone rang out. "I gotta take this."

And he hurried to his office.

"Oh, yum," Chris yammered, devouring the tofu with the gusto of a Thanksgiving glutton. "Yum! Yum!" Then rising from the table, he let out the loudest burp. "For the Dalai Lama."

"Tsk, tsk," his mother tsked, "you call that gratitude?"

He picked up his plate. "You call that food?"

"Put it down, please. You put that down, Christopher, right now."

"Fine." Obeying without thinking, he let the plate fall, and it shattered on the floor.

"Thank you, universe," Val made herself say, and kept eating, thinking the boys would return to their senses and the table. But they didn't return. "Oh, universe," she said, trying to stay positive, "what the hell?"

The next day, Chris went online and bought a new set of dishes—a large collection—with a nice Tibetan pattern. And during lunch (tofu turkey leftovers) he sincerely apologized to his well-meaning mother. She sincerely accepted his apology and told him to move, permanently, into the cottage.

"Before Solstice," she said. "That's a good time to begin anew."

"I figured you'd say that. And, um, yeah, it's probably a good idea."

"Find a stupid roommate," his father said. "Get a renter to pay your bills. And your tuition. Have you applied to UMD or Scholastica yet?"

"No, not yet."

Having just evicted her son, Val spoke extra motherly. "Honey Bear, I know an old nun at Saint Scholastica who practices natural healing. I think Scholastica has a good mix of ancient and modern opportunities. It would be a fine education, Topher, especially if you decide to become a teacher."

"A teacher? Me?"

She nodded. "Yeah. You. A teacher."

"Or even a professor," Joe said, messing the boy's hair. "I can totally see it. Professor Lake. No mistake!"

"What would I teach?"

"Business," Joe said.

"Art," Val said. "Or literature. You have an expressive spirit that demands expression."

"Hmm," Chris thought. "Well, if I were to become a teacher, I'd probably teach earth science. Trees, rocks, water, fish. You know, things that make sense."

"There's good money in science," Joe said.

The rich young man looked his father in the eye. "To be honest, I don't really care about money. I just need enough to survive."

"Good boy," Val said. "Be grateful for everything."

"Okay, Mom."

"And never take less than market value."

"Okay, Dad."

"And I'm still mad," Joe added, "that you were never able to sell that cottage. I think you made it too medieval."

Chapter Sixty-One

Advent is an adventure of waiting, of awaiting the arrival of the kingliest of kingdoms, and Christopher couldn't wait to move out of his parents' house and establish his own kingdom on earth. All of his worldly possessions fit easily into the rooms of the stone cottage; and he purchased one more item from the internet to make the place even more medieval: a suit of armor. It was shiny, and it fit him, but it wasn't real. It was a theater costume, tinkered from aluminum.

Probably made of beer cans.

Disgusted, the aspirant knight tossed the clattering garment into the closet and slammed the door. He sat on the cold stone floor, wondering how he could be such an idiot. He should have known better than to buy a piece of crap from an online seller named "Garyteed Goode."

"What am I even doing? With my life?"

He slept on the floor that night, and the next night. He stopped eating. He let the phone ring and didn't check his messages.

Two weeks before Christmas, Pixie and Trevor, wearing Santa hats, came *fa-la-la-ing* on the snowy steps, trying to give Christopher some holiday cheer. He slowly arose and opened the door, but when they sang, "*Bring me flesh and bring me wine*," he closed it again.

Chris laid down beneath the window in the living room, waiting and waiting—for what? He left the purple drapes open, and just kept lying on the floor.

Eventually, in the middle of a starry starless night, the first line of a poem or song infused his mind—*Born of earth, haunted by the heavenly*—and the aspirant knight yawned the words away, having no desire to write them down on the last sheet of stationary remaining from his birthday gift of long ago. Christopher just kept lying on the floor, shivering, wasting away.

Chapter Sixty-Two

"Party! Parrtyy dowwn!"

Moosehead and Skunk tracked snow into the cottage and handed Chris a whiskey bottle (half full) and yelled, "Sacramento! You own a freaking house!"

"I do?"

Skunk lifted his friend from the floor and stammered, "I should buy-buy a house myself. I've saved ah-ah few hundred dollars!"

"Oh. Um, welcome, guys." Chris sniffed the whiskey, made a funny face, and took a gulp. He choked and coughed, eyes watering, but that first swig did wonders to his mood, the booze oozing into his brain. "Goodness gracious." He took another gulp. "Heck yeah, I own a house!"

The party really got going when some hockey players

burst through the door. They had a case of beer and plenty of girlfriends, one of whom tried to swing from the chandelier. Emo music soon filled the cottage, along with more students from East, all of them full of the ecstasy of angst and the agony of cheap booze. By midnight, there were a hundred uninvited guests.

"Party! Party!"

Moosehead and Skunk ordered pizzas (with Chris's credit card) and wings and ribs and spaghetti. Someone else ordered Mexican. And burgers and fries and shakes. And around midnight, Chris squeezed into his suit of armor and began jangle-dancing while the revelers cheered and smacked his metallic ass, nobody noticing how the aurora borealis was turning the living-room window into living stained-glass.

"Parrrtyy dowwwnn!!"

Chris clanked upon a chair, gasping for breath through his knight's helmet. He slid it off to give a speech—thinking he should say something profound about the approach of Christmas, something joyful and spiritual to inspire his fellow lords and ladies—and then he became deathly pale, convulsed, and filled his helmet with barf.

"Chug, chug, chug!" the revelers said, going about their merry way.

Chapter Sixty-Three

With Christmas another day closer, more adventing light streamed through the windows upon Christopher wallowing in filth. Not only his own filth, but the garbage of his “guests.” There was rib sauce on chairs, pasta sauce on walls, and various multi-colored things oozing on the floor.

Gonna be sick again, Chris thought, struggling to stand. *Gonna be sick forever?*

His head pounded with the after-curse of whiskey, beer, wine, vodka, tequila, and whatever else had been offered to him. Chris recalled something about a cop and a call from his parents—it was all a buzzing, painful blur—and another mess.

Sickly, but determined, he worked on the cottage for several hours, until it looked respectable again, and the last thing put in its place was the suit of armor. He gave it a shower, figuring rust was better than barf, then carried the lifeless life of the party to the closet and propped it in a corner. *Maybe I should junk it?* As he stood deciding, he noticed a box of books, those old cherished gifts from Terra and Professor Corwin—poems, stories, and lives of death-defying lovers and heroes.

I'll read 'em all, he thought, dragging the dusty box into the living room toward a scarlet loveseat. *This time, I really will.*

Chapter Sixty-Four

Christmas morning, Christopher shaved, bathed, and dressed in his holy-day best. He left the clean stone cottage and stomped through the snow to Majestic. With a bare hand he brushed off the windshield, climbed inside, mouthed a prayer, and turned the key. "Please start, please start, please..." The car sparked, sputtered, and died. He tried again. The car sparked, sputtered, and groaned to life. "Good!" It began slowly moving through snow drifts in the driveway and plowed forward toward the road, while Chris began singing in his soul, almost joyfully, *Noelle.*

Noelle...Noelle. Noelle...Noelle! Born is the Kinggg of—oh, man, I don't feel so good.

The hungover knight accelerated up the hill and swerved on a patch of ice—*Yikes*—he hazily remembered driver's ed again and carefully climbed the slippery slope toward Skyline and Holy Spirit. In the rearview mirror he caught a glimpse of Lake Superior, unfrozen this year, the surface sparkling like so many silver bells. "The lake is alive!" he sang out loud, "with the sound of—with the sound of—" *Oh, man, don't barf again.*

The image of silver-belled Superior made him recall the movie he'd seen at The Barn Theater, and he was hoping to see the Mudgett family at Mass, thinking maybe they'd invite him to the farm for a Christmas feast, so much goat stew, goat milk, goat yogurt, and goat chocolate, and suddenly a surge of happiness and nausea overwhelmed him—he got lightheaded and almost fainted—and ran a red light.

Oh, man...

Chris hit the brakes and skidded to the side of the road, nearly crashing into a building, Saint Mary Star of the Sea. He tried to back up, wheels spinning and spinning. Majestic was stuck near the stairway. "Oh, great. Just great." Chris killed the engine, rolled down the window, and tried to breathe calmly. *I need a tow truck.* But he hadn't brought his phone. "I need a new brain," he muttered. "One that does what it should."

An old woman in a blue parka opened the church door and peered down at him, saying, "Look what you did!"

Oh, crap. Gonna call the cops? What if she calls the same cop that broke up my party?

The old woman smiled and waved, beckoning him inside as if parking near the stairs was perfectly acceptable. "Happens all the time," she said.

"Um, okay." Chris abandoned Majestic and began climbing the salty stairs. He paused for a while at the entrance, still feeling sickly from his indulgences, and continued forward through the door. Immediately the young knight was greeted by an angel holding a large seashell, offering sparkling holy water. Chris wondered if the water was from Lake Superior and blessed beyond its depths. He dipped a pale, trembling finger, crossed himself, and shuffled into a back pew. *Wow, look at that. I've never seen that before.* Gold and purple lights from the windows crowned the heads of all the worshippers.

With renewed reverence, Chris sang the hymns and responded to the Scriptures. He even said, "Thanks be to God" and "Praise to you, Lord Jesus Christ."

When it was time for Communion, Christopher knelt and watched everyone else ascend to receive. He felt cursed and blessed and confused as usual, and he glanced at a lovely young woman returning from the altar. Her face was radiant. He had to blink his eyes.

The woman knelt in a middle row and disappeared.

Wait a sec, wait a sec. I know—

Chris lurched into the aisle and rushed to the center of the church, scooting into the pew and kneeling beside her. A thousand words of adoration spirited on the tip of his tongue, rendering him almost speechless.

"*The world is charged—*" he began.

"*—with the grandeur of God,*" Terra answered. She turned to him, her face all tears. "My mother is very ill. She's in the hospital across the street. Stay with me, Christopher, okay?"

"For sure."

The two of them stayed in the church until it was empty. Chris took Terra's hand and she rested her head on his shoulder.

"What's wrong with your mother?"

"Pancreatic cancer."

"Is that term—" he said, unable to finish.

"Terminal, yes," Terra said. "We're almost at the end."

"I'm sorry to hear that. I'm really sorry."

"The doctors and nurses are doing their best, but it's not enough. All she does is suffer. I can't bear it. My mother was the strongest person in the world. Now she can't eat or drink. She can barely speak. Every breath seems to be killing her. And my father is—my father is not here. I have a horrible feeling he's dead. Probably been dead for a long time."

"Terra...Terra..."

Christopher gently touched her face, brushing away some of the tears. Then he looked up and glared at the murals on the ceiling, artwork showing the Savior feeding, healing, even raising the dead, perfectly capable of anything. *And yet, Mrs. Corwin suffers, and Terra suffers. Suffering like hell.*

"Chris, will you go with me to the hospital? She's in the hospice unit."

"Of course," he said, rising. "Let's go."

Chapter Sixty-Five

All bundled up in her deathbed, Mrs. Corwin opened an eye and turned her head slightly. "Is that...is that..." she rasped, "who I hope it is?"

Chris approached the bed shyly, like a little kid.

"Oh, my." Mrs. Corwin opened her other eye and attempted to lift her skeletal hand. She couldn't lift it, but smiled anyway. "Christopher Lake. The great reader. Remember?"

His mind searched for the best words, for something soothing, preferably profound. He bowed in silence and kissed Mrs. Corwin on the forehead.

"Old-school...romantic," she said, a lone tear dribbling down her translucent face. The dying woman closed her eyes with a sense of finality, and the room went silent.

Chris knelt and made the Sign of the Cross, believing Mrs. Corwin had passed away. He whispered, "She was a great person."

"She's just resting," Terra said. "She's still with us. Still breathing."

"Oh, sorry. I thought she was gone." Chris stood and swiped at his tears. His nose was flowing as well and he wiped it with his shirt. *So gross.* This wasn't how he wanted Terra to see him after so many years. When he'd recognized her in Star of the Sea, it seemed like a sign that was also a promise. That's why he'd run down the aisle toward her, as if his whole life had been signaling for that moment of present and future happiness. Now he glared out the window at Lake Superior, noticing how it had shape-shifted with coils of mist rising like a fire-breathing serpent, approaching the hillside as if laying claim to everything.

No.

No, you can't have her.

Christopher whirled and returned to Mrs. Corwin's side. He whispered, "Is there anything I can get for you? Just say the word, and I'll get it. I'll go to any store in town, or out of town. Anything you want. Do you want chocolates? Special gourmet coffee? Roses?"

Terra reminded him, "It's Christmas. The stores are closed."

"I don't care. I'll break in."

"Oh, yes." Mrs. Corwin opened her eyes. "I do want. Something."

"Name it," Chris said. "Anything."

She lifted her hand and reached out, trembling, for Chris's hand. "Oh. I want," she said, "to apologize."

"Apologize? What for?"

"At the dance...long ago...I said you'd hurt us."

"Well, you were just being a protective mom. It's okay."

Mrs. Corwin's eyes were so sunken, yet soft and glistening as a newborn's. "I was wrong," she said. "You're helping...us."

"I'm trying."

Around the clock, Chris stayed in the hospice. He sat silently, giving space for Terra and her mom to converse. It was so difficult for Mrs. Corwin to speak, taking all her energy, each precious word almost killing her. And when the dying woman was sleeping, Chris whispered to the girl he'd always loved.

"How's your grandfather? Funny and wise as ever? His box of books inspired me to go to Mass today. And now I'm here with you."

Terra's face revealed a sad happiness, and she hesitated to speak, not wanting to hurt Chris with the sad part of the news.

"Just tell me."

"Grandfather passed away. Last year."

Silvenshine...Chris thought, unable to speak, tears falling. *Silvenshine*...

"It was a good death," Terra said. "His heart was clean. There were angels at his bedside."

"Angels? For real?"

"Yes."

"I believe it." Christopher took a deep breath. "You know, I always wanted to contact you and keep up with everything in your life."

"Same," she said, touching his face. "And thank you for being here now."

For the next two weeks, Chris attended to the Corwins, rarely leaving the hospital room. Snow fell almost every day, whitening the bleakness out the window, and Chris read from a book that made the dying woman happy. *Canterbury Tales*. The first few tales he read quickly, thinking Mrs. Corwin wouldn't make it to the end. However, her attention eventually increased, and she was able to sit up. Chris slowed his cadence for the last chapters and wondered if perhaps he was part of a miracle.

When the nurses or doctors were in the room, Chris and Terra sometimes went out to the hallway for a walk, stretching their legs and chatting about their shared memories of timeless moments in the library, and in the gardens, and along the shoreline. "Remember that time you led me to Purgatory?" "Of course, you dork." Holding hands, they wandered around the hospital acting like an inseparable couple, joking, laughing, sharing tears.

Mrs. Corwin hung on into January, all the way to Epiphany, while the young knight kept reading to her, finishing in a flourish the final tale, the Parson's homily for reaching Heaven.

"The end," Chris said, gently closing the book.

"Great...story," she rasped. "I loved it. Now call...the priest. Now."

In that hour, while luminous snowflakes fluttered against the window, Mrs. Corwin said, "God be with you" to Terra and Christopher, made her final confession, then fell into a deep sleep, the deepest of her life. When the priest left the room, Terra wasn't sure what was next. Crying, trying to smile for the sake of faith, she climbed into the bed and stroked her mother's hair, whispering prayers, forgiving everything, thankful for everything, and just loving her mother to eternity.

Chris stood nearby, trying to be a strong presence—although his knees began to shake. "I should help you," he said, not wanting to say what was next. "Make funeral arrangements." He reached for his phone. "Who do I call?"

Terra's tears fell on her mother's shoulder. "I wish...you

could call my father."

"I think you said he swore off phones—even before he left home."

"Yeah. He left no tech trail at all. And it's been so long now, I'm sure he's—"

"Alive, and I'll find him," Chris said. He leaned over the bed and took her hand. "I promise you, Terra. I'll find your father. You'll see."

"I will?" She searched his promising eyes. "We don't know what country he's in. It could be anywhere—anywhere with a place of pilgrimage."

"If he's living in a hobbit monastery in New Zealand, I'll find him."

A smile crossed Terra's sad face. "A hobbit monastery?"

"Yeah."

She almost laughed. "There are no hobbit monasteries, you dork."

"Yeah, but I'm just saying. If such a place existed, and your father happened to be there, I'd find him. Do you carry a photo of him?"

"In my tote bag, always." Terra reached over to a chair, fished around in the tote, and pulled out the picture. "Here it is. But you don't have time to travel. Mother will be gone soon. You can't carry my father's pic across the whole world."

Chris admired Victor Corwin's pious, intelligent face. "With some help, I can."

Chapter Sixty-Six

It will flame out, like shining from shook foil...

Chris rushed into his father's office. "Can I rent all your computers?" The rich young man pulled out his wallet. "Name your price, Dad. I need all your office equipment to help the Corwins."

"Topher, sweetheart!" Val cried, entering the room. "We've missed you. How are things at the hospice?"

"Not good. Terrible. I mean—"

"Oh, sweetie. I'm sorry."

Chris emptied his wallet, slapping the cash on his father's desk. "If you need more, I'll go to the ATM."

"Hmm." Picking up the money and slowly counting it, Joe scoffed at the offer. "Seven hundred and thirty dollars? Don't be foolish. Son. If you're helping people you love, then my office and everything I have is yours. For free."

"Thanks, Dad. I appreciate it."

"Here. Take your cash. And don't carry so much around. Invest it."

"Okay, Dad."

"Oh, sweetie." Val lunged forward and gave Chris a big hug. "Are you hungry? I made a fruitcake. With veggies. You'll love it."

"Maybe later, Mom. Thanks." Chris sat at a desk, fired up a computer, dialed his cell, and spoke urgently into the phone. "Pix, hey! I need your help. Can you hurry over to my parents' house? Yeah? You can? Awesome! And please bring Trevor. Yes, I really said that. And bring your computers."

Chris called up Moosehead and Skunk as well, asking for their help, even though he wondered if they'd be more trouble than help. The two appeared almost instantly, stomping into the house with backpacks stuffed with all the electronics they'd owned since childhood. They took off their snowy boots and coats, and said in unison, "Got anything to eat?"

"Careful what you ask for," Chris said, watching his mother dash toward the kitchen. "Okay, guys, let's get to work."

Just then the doorbell rang and the door flung open. It

was Pixie and Trevor, the latter entering first, proclaiming, "I've already infused this endeavor—whatever it is—with powerful prayers."

"Thanks, Trev," Chris said, slapping him on the back.

"Haha," he replied. "No glasses to break. I love these contact lenses."

"Great. Let's get focused."

The group gathered in Joe's office—with posters of the Grateful Dead watching them—and sent out Victor Corwin's photograph and information. Trevor was something of a techie and extremely helpful in locating pilgrimage sites and corresponding hostels. From Jerusalem to Alexandria to Lourdes to Fatima to Patmos to every place on earth associated with the heavenly, the group sent out their plea for help.

"HAVE YOU SEEN THIS MAN? HIS WIFE IS DYING AND HE MUST RETURN HOME. PLEASE RESPOND TO THIS EMAIL OR CALL THE NUMBER BELOW. REWARD OFFERED."

Trevor suggested sending the message in multiple languages and gave everyone the link for translations. Pixie cooed, "That's pretty dang smart." And that inspired Trevor to basically take over the project. He showed Moosehead and Skunk how to be more efficient, beginning by taking away their video games. "That's better," he said, "no more multi-tasking. Stay on mission. Send the message. Send it!"

Around the world the message flew, imploring good-hearted souls to help bless a suffering family. And within an hour, there were responses.

"Here's one from Croatia," Moosehead said. "It says the hostel has been taken over by a hotel, and do we want to rent it—dirty cheap. That's what it says—dirty cheap."

"Delete," Chris said, not looking up from his screen.

"Just got an email from Brazil," Pixie said. "I had a feeling they'd respond, because of my bird Rio, and that's how God has been working lately, but anyway, it's just an ad for some miracle oil. Anyone want miracle oil?"

Trevor shook his head. "We're getting junk replies. Nothing but junk so far."

"I just got-got a message from Wales!" Skunk yelled. "We-we won a lottery! We-we just need to send a deposit!"

"Delete," Chris said, not looking up.

The internet frustration continued for several hours. Not a single response was promising. Joe eventually joined the group and sent out hundreds of emails from his business account, thinking that would add credibility—to no avail. "I'm guessing most people think we're trying to scam them. And some of them want to scam us."

"What's the solution?" Chris said. "There has to be a better way." The boy's eyes were watering at the thought of disappointing Terra.

"I don't know, son. Direct mailings are tough, especially digital cold calls."

"Damn!" Moosehead said, watching Val enter with a tray of veggie fruitcake and mugs of tea. "Sorry about my language, but I'm starving. That stuff edible?"

"I'll say Grace," Trevor said. "Don't freak out. I'll say it quick." Everyone bowed their heads, even the old hippies, and the moment the prayer ended Christopher stood and said, "I'm going to the bookstore. I'll be right back."

"The brick bookstore?" Pixie asked, "where I bought your birthday present?"

"Yep. That's the one."

Joe muttered, "There's no time to study books now. Seems like a bad plan, at this stage, to waste time on books."

Chris hurried to the door and left without looking back.

"He isn't going for books," Pixie said. "Just wait, you'll see. It's a good plan."

Within thirty minutes, the young man returned with a ton of fancy stationary, a golden pen, formal envelopes, and wax. "Mom," he said. "What's the best essential oil I can mix with the wax? You know, something irresistible."

"Like a potion? Hmm." Val was thrilled to be asked such a question. "You want me to make a love potion?"

"No, no." Chris placed all the materials on a desk.

"Not a potion. I just want everyone receiving a letter to feel special. I want them to open the letters already feeling happy, connected, a part of the plan."

"You-you have a new-new plan?" Skunk asked.

"Whatever," Moosehead whispered. "Did you bring any burgers or anything?"

Sigh. "Didn't you just eat?"

"Sort of."

"You know," Joe said, "an essential oil that always makes me happy is frankincense."

"Oh, yes," Val said, clapping, "and I'll mix it with myrrh."

"Hope you have those oils stocked in the house," Chris said. "We don't have time for more shopping." He sat the desk and leaned over the materials, ready to begin again.

"Of course, sweetie. I'll be right back."

After two seconds, Moosehead snorted, "Yup. I'm still hungry."

"Fine. Here's fifty dollars." Chris handed over the cash. "Order some burgers or pizza or whatever."

"Pizza is edible," Moosehead declared. "With no veggies."

"Pepperoni," Trevor said, "with mushrooms and black olives. That's Pixie's favorite."

"Your favorite, too," she cooed.

"If you kiss-kiss," Skunk said, "I'm outta here."

"Nobody's kissing nobody," Pixie replied. "We're here to work."

The rest of the night, while others sent out emails, Christopher handwrote a thousand letters. Every few hours, he called Terra to check on her, and to ask about her mother's condition, but otherwise he worked without stopping, writing personal notes that went something like this:

To the Church of the Nativity in Bethlehem,

Greetings from a land holy in its own way—northern Minnesota. Did you know we have mountain lions? You should visit. The people (and the lions, for the most part) are very nice.

Please take a minute and look at the enclosed picture. That's Victor Corwin. His wife is dying. His daughter is distraught. He must return home immediately.

Would you kindly show this to everyone in your church?

And call the number below if you have any info.

God be with you.

Kindest regards,

Christopher (friend of the family) Lake

He wrote letter after letter, even when his hand went numb, even after it regained feeling and felt broken. He welcomed the pain and would not relax, thinking about the poor souls in the hospice. And he sealed every envelope with red wax infused with frankincense and myrrh.

In the morning, when the others were slumped in various chairs and snoring, Christopher went to Fed-Ex to have the world-wide mailings delivered the fastest way possible. A nice bald guy behind the counter said, "This is crazy, kid. We've never had an order for so much money. You could send these three-day instead of overnight. You sure about this?"

"I'm sure," Chris said, writing the check. He calculated in his head that this expense, along with the reward money, would pretty much deplete his savings. "Perfect," he said, and ambled across the street to the Superior Café to buy breakfast to bring home for his fellow workers.

Chapter Sixty-Seven

Generations have trod, have trod, have trod...

One of the hand-written letters was delivered to a Benedictine monastery near Canterbury, and one day later a bearded man dressed like a medieval peasant appeared in the hospice above the harbor. He entered the room of his beautiful wife and daughter, his eyes sparkling with sorrow.

"Hello, loves," he whispered guiltily.

Terra was sleeping in a chair. Victor slowly approached and kissed her forehead, then limped over to the bed where his wife was passing away. He knelt, prayed, and wept.

Christopher stood by the window, feeling mixed emotions about this apparent miracle. He'd worked beyond his strength to make this moment happen, and now a surge of anger began filling his soul, darkening the vision of reunification. *Vic thinks he can show up and blabber about love? After leaving them loveless all these years?*

Mrs. Corwin opened her eyes. "Hello...love."

"I'm sorry," Victor said, remaining on his knees. "More than sorry. I never meant to go away and not return. I just got lost in finding myself. I just—"

"Angels..." Mrs. Corwin said, "...brought you back."

"Angels, yes." Victor leaned closer to his wife. "I never wanted to be away from my family. Never for a moment. But I had to be penitent. I felt called, so I went, and I walked—all over the world—as if I could pay in pounds of flesh and pain for having made the world a worse place. All I ever wanted was to make it better."

Terra awoke. "Father?" Thinking it might be a dream, she hesitated for a moment, glanced at her mom who was nodding yes, then rushed forward to give her father a hug. "You're here! It's really you!"

"It's really me."

"And mom's awake!"

She hugged them both, then turned to Christopher, her glowing face and eyes proclaiming: *You did it!*

His soul answered: *I love you*. And he almost said it.

"When I was returning," Victor told his wife, stroking her hair, "way out over the ocean, I prayed the plane to be quicker than light. I wanted to be here instantaneously.

And I began thinking about our wedding in that little chapel near Sacramento. The old priest with his ancient voice, the chanting, the incense—"

She smiled. "And you…so handsome."

"I was all nerves, while you stood calmly at the altar, taking your place in Heaven."

"Sweet…talker." Mrs. Corwin laughed painfully, her eyes informing Victor that this was the end.

His tears fell on her gray and radiant hair, and he gave his wife a last kiss, gentle, passionate, perfectly sad.

"Forgiven," she said, trailing off, "and…now…"

"Mom," Terra pleaded, "don't leave us. Not yet. Please. Dad promises to stay this time."

"Yes," Victor said, reaching for both of their hands. "I promise. I promise."

Chapter Sixty-Eight

The funeral Mass for Mrs. Corwin was held in the upper room of the cathedral. Christopher sat in the back, dressed in black, and he knelt, and stood, and prayed, the Latin feeling both natural and supernatural. The chapel was as lovely as he'd imagined—oak wood beams, artistic statuary, stone altar, rose windows—everything aligned with the sturdiness of light. When Terra and her father went up to the Communion rail, Chris vowed that he'd be with them in time.

Lux Christi, he heard in his head.

Deo gratias, he replied. *Deo gratias...times infinity.*

Long after the Mass, when everyone else was downstairs or gone home, Chris and Terra sat alone near the open casket, their clothes becoming royal purple as waves of sunlight washed through a sunset window.

"She seems to be floating," Terra said. "So peaceful, so peaceful. Seven heavens, Mom. Float through them all."

Christopher kept silent, hoping his presence was saying everything to the girl he loved. Each moment felt like a poem too real to be written in this world, and his heart was both heavy and weightless. He glanced outside and saw lights on the lake dancing like a borealis of a better dream.

He fathers-forth whose beauty is past change...

"Terra," he finally said, "your father sought me out after the final blessing. He hugged me, thanked me for the letter, and said I was a special friend of the family."

"I know. I saw it."

Terra closed her eyes, and kept them shut for a while, making Chris worry that he'd said too much, that he was already ruining things.

"It's not true," Terra said, opening her eyes and taking his hand. "You're not a special friend of the family. You're a part of the family." She smiled a radiance that kissed his soul. "And always will be."

About the Author

David Athey is the author of many books, including the Florida comedy *Iggy in Paradise*. He has published more than 200 poems, stories, essays, and reviews in magazines and literary journals such as *Christianity & Literature, Berkeley Fiction Review, Harvard Review, Palm Beach Illustrated, Tampa Review,* and *Notre Dame Magazine*. Athey is an award-winning professor at Palm Beach Atlantic University and has also served as Artist-in-Residence at the Alexander W. Dreyfoos School of the Arts.

Visit David Athey's author page at Amazon.com

Books by David Athey

ART is for THE ARTIST

May these meditations inspire and encourage you to write your best and make beautiful art.

Everything in creation sings of God's wild creativity.

Soulful art evokes an "Immanuel moment," a sense that God is with us.

Beauty will save us from the world.

THE COUNT OF TRINITY

Hidden away in the mountains is a sort of medieval community of farmers, artists, and monks, minding their own business and preparing to celebrate the grand wedding of their "royal couple."

However, the community finds itself under attack by mysterious forces bent on destroying everything.

The Count of Trinity is poetic, romantic, and funny, full of natural and supernatural adventure.

IGGY IN PARADISE

When a handsome young Alaskan arrives in Florida, hailed by the internet as "The Greatest Salesman in the World," all hell breaks loose, including a pirate limo driver, a talking iguana, mermaids that work for FOMA (the Fountain of Middle Age) and two or three of the strangest love stories you've ever witnessed, because, well, Florida. Only in Florida will a gang of dentists battle a volunteer SWAT team while a handsome Alaskan raps bad poetry in an exploding house for love, honor, and to impress both Aphrodite and a semi-pro BINGO player named Daphne.

THE PILGRIM

These poems, written in Minnesota and Florida, are full of images of paradise.

Whether the heavenly things of earth break our hearts or mend them, they are meant to lead us higher.

SEVENTY: FLASH FICTION STORIES

All of the characters in Athey's stories are infused with a grace of light in a world of pain, suffering, beauty, love, and redemption.

THE GLIMMERING KID

In the wilderness town of Glimmering, Minnesota, a boy named Albertus goes on a double quest: to find treasure for his mom and for himself. It's his mom's birthday, so the boy will risk battling a Dragon, a Sasquatch, and even some Badgers that are somewhat human. Oh, and there's also a girl named Lily Frank who makes his stomach hurt, and an international gem thief named Dakota Stalinova who parachutes upon Minnesota to steal the treasure. Let us hope Albertus can prevail. Oh no! Here come the thieving Badgers, proclaiming, "We is invincible! We is! We is!"

Fast-paced and wildly humorous, *The Glimmering Kid* will brighten your day (and Mom will like it too).

ELEVEN MANATEES

The quintessence of poetry, perhaps, is the humble haiku. Three little lines, a handful of syllables, a smidge of aesthetics, and there is the whole universe—in an earthy, heavenly hint.

lilies on the moon
a garden in the lake
after the hurricane

eleven manatees
floating, dreaming
christmas eve

THAT & THIS

This eclectic collection has that: fiction, nonfiction, poetry, and drama.

Stories: about a cat-lady detective in Florida; a parking-ramp attendant in Moscow (Idaho) who gets attacked by bearded maniacs; a teacher who discovers the dangers of cell phones and Flannery O'Connor...

Essays: about a Christmas iguana; the greatness of haiku; dealing with death; the glories of the Church.

Poems: about creativity and prayer; Little Havana; the Everglades and Heaven.

Plays: about Cain and Shakespeare.

ABOVE THE HARBOR

Young Christopher Lake is enthralled by life along the coast of majestic Lake Superior. He is something of a mystic, a talented writer and musician. Searching for a muse and more, he engages in a series of awkward dates with three amazing girls and is ultimately haunted by the heavens to deepen his life in love.

Poetic, romantic, and humorous, *Above the Harbor* is a coming-of-age pilgrimage through the wilderness of nature, human relationships, and the strange wild beauty of the soul.

THE STRAW THAT HEALED THE CAMEL'S BACK

Imagine being the camel who carried the Christmas gift of gold to Bethlehem. Imagine how heavy the gold must have been—heavy enough to break a camel's back! Poor Trubba Drom is a very troublesome beast. He likes to bellow, burp, and spit at everyone, always making a mess of everything. Yet he was chosen to deliver treasure to the King. Follow along as Trubba Drom journeys to Bethlehem and learns the true meaning of Christmas (which includes not bellowing, burping, or spitting).

For kids of all ages.

Beautifully illustrated by Alice Browning.

Made in the USA
Middletown, DE
05 March 2025

72042030R00157